The
Lemurian

Darin Williams

Outskirts Press, Inc.
Denver, Colorado

The Lemurian
All Rights Reserved.

Outskirts Press, Inc.
http://www.outskirtspress.com

ISBN: 978-1-4327-2803-8

Library of Congress Control Number: 2008931883

Outskirts Press and the "OP" logo are trademarks belonging to Outskirts Press, Inc.

PRINTED IN THE UNITED STATES OF AMERICA

Acknowledgement

This book would never had been started without the influence and inspiration of my Grandfather, Charles Marvin Williams, or 'Gramps' as our family warmly called him. His stories, curiosity and sense of humor, coupled with his strength of character, were a perfect blend for a child to look up to. He is greatly missed.

The Lemurian would still be stuffed in a binder collecting dust, if I hadn't had the support and encouragement of my family and some of my closest and dearest friends. To them, I am truly grateful, as their enthusiasm has inspired me to continue writing the forthcoming series of *The Lemurian*.

Thank you also to Bethany Williams for my photo on the back cover.

"Dreams are located just beyond our fingertips for a reason. If we keep stretching, we will grow enough to reach them and genuinely appreciate them"

Darin Williams

Chapter 1

Like minuscule icicles piercing her flesh at random on her body, this unexplainable sensation was returning. Mya wasn't frightened of it; she had been experiencing these strange feelings since puberty. Each time stronger, each time odd things happened around her. Though she never was able to control it, she still tried.

Each 'sting' made a rippling effect, like a hailstone falling into a pond. She could feel each hair on her body begin to straighten, her sensitivity was acute, the frequency of 'stings' was increasing. Something was very different about this time. The feeling began to engulf her senses, enhancing not smothering. Soon her whole body seemed to be humming from the inside out, like a tuning fork that had just been struck. Amazingly, this overpowering feeling wasn't even noticed by her best friend Allison, sitting only a few feet from her.

The two had been best friends since college, sharing their most intimate secrets with each other, vacationing together, helping each other in any situation, yet Mya couldn't bring herself to share this one thing, she felt like a freak. Because of the peculiarness of this phase, she began to withdraw, almost not hearing anything Allison was saying. That, however, was something her friend picked up on.

"Are you all right Mya? You seemed to have just drifted into your own little world!"

"Sorry Allison, I just began to realize I hadn't finished my presentation handouts for the Maxwell pitch tomorrow. Maybe I should get back home and get it all together before it gets late."

Allison knew Mya was a perfectionist when it came to work. She was very focused and always prepared early. Something seemed to pre-occupy Mya and it wasn't work, but she didn't press to get it out of her, she knew that Mya knew she wasn't buying it. Her friend was the most outgoing, driven and flirtatious individual she knew, but at the moment very withdrawn and almost evasive.

There was an ancient artifacts show touring through their city called 'Lost Memories in Time'. Allison thought this would be a sure fire way to bring her buddy out of her funk, so later that afternoon she called and insisted Mya come with her, she would pick her up at 4:30. Feeling guilty for how she treated her earlier, Mya agreed.

When she arrived, Allison looked more like she was going to a club than a museum. She informed Mya that they were stopping for martinis to relax first; they both laughed.

Sinatra tunes flowed from a piano in a dark corner of the lounge; the cool martinis slid down their throats like liquid silver, smooth and rich. Allison's scheme paid off. Mya was much more relaxed, back to her playful and flirty self. They walked arm in arm to the museum, only two blocks away; enjoying the warm evening air, giggling and making passes at people walking by. They both had a pretty good buzz going, though hardly drunk.

As they entered the museum foyer they settled down as not to arouse undue attention. Behind the guard desk was a small TV tuned to a sports event, a wastepaper basket sat next to it. Mya walked over to toss a tissue in but it fell short. As she bent down to pick it up she noticed the TV image fade to snow, indicating some type of electrical interference. When she moved away, it cleared up. She hoped it was only a coincidence.

Allison had already gone through the metal detector gate and was calling for her to hurry. As she walked through, Mya glanced up to the security monitor overhead and noticed a glitch or a skip just as she passed through. The guard happened to find it peculiar too and politely asked that she walk through again. Mya's heart was now racing; did he know something was going on with her? Once again the monitor skipped just as she passed through, she definitely saw it. The guard slapped the side of it calling a piece of crap. Mya knew better, it was caused by the phase. The metal detector didn't beep and he let her pass.

Allison was much more interested in ancient civilizations than Mya, but when they entered the wing that displayed the stones, jewelry, and ritual artifacts, Mya felt a huge wave of energy engulf her and go straight to her soul.

As she approached an uncovered display, she realized that the stones began to vibrate and emit different harmonic tones. When she backed up, they stopped. With her heart racing and her mind reeling with questions and uncertainty, Mya edged closer; again the stone began to sing.

"Allison! Over here, do you hear that?"

"Hear what?" Asked Allison. The only thing her friend could hear was a tour guide reciting a script to a group of retirees. This was no ordinary phase.

Chapter 2

Seth had been studying and preparing for this journey for what seemed like half of his young life, but it had actually only been about three years. Everyone knew how courageous he was, how well trained in the Mysteries, but nobody could possibly know how excited he really was. It was very rare for anyone in this day and time to venture to the surface and be seen, let alone live amongst the <u>profane</u> civilizations above. He, like his ancestors, was from a most secret tribe, a most sacred culture; one that must not be discovered and diluted.

When the earliest settlers came to their region a few hundred years ago, some of the village's elders went into their towns and traded gold nuggets for various goods hoping to learn more about the new neighbors. The townspeople were also curious. Why would these 'strange' Indians trade large nuggets of gold for goods worth a fraction of its value? Where did they live? No one could ever find a trace of a village. Those who tried to follow them either got lost or fled the forest with frantic tales of strange happenings when they ventured too deep. Most of all where was all of that gold coming from?

The entire village was readying for a grand ceremony. Elders from other tribes came to assist in the rituals. Ancient mantras and sacrament would be performed to protect his pure mind, thought and powers. After the ceremony and the feasting, there were only the final tests of his resolve that would allow his passage to the surface.

The night before his departure, Seth lay on an altar like bed, lined with large tropical leaves and surrounded by a ring of ritual stones and burning incense.

Twelve young women, one from each of the orders, anointed his long body with a highly magnetized oil, blessed from each elder. He would be left alone for twelve hours to rest and finish preparing his mind for the journey.

The night had passed quickly, Seth heard someone approaching. It was Kira, the Highest Elder, and two children. They brought the clothing he was to wear along with the currency he needed to survive in his new world.

He still didn't agree with the need for money; in his world everyone graciously shared all things with each other. One need not bribe or have to give up ones valuables in exchange for food, clothing or shelter. However he had to accept it to blend in successfully.

The clothes felt restrictive to him, a pair of long pants, flannel shirt and a wide brimmed hat that covered his large forehead, a feature that identified his kind. The boots hurt his feet so much that he decided to wear his sandals and carry his boots in his backpack. He looked just like one of the many hikers they had watched pass through the forest.

Finally, Kira placed a pendant around his neck. Very simple looking, a small crystalline stone wrapped tightly in a green leaf, and suspended by a leather strand; all had been soaking in the same magnetized oil that he had been anointed with.

"You must never take this off." She warned him. "This will help protect the abilities that you have mastered so well, against their machines that interfere with your senses."

"Elder Kira, I will guard it with my very soul." Assured Seth.

"May our ancestors guide and protect you, health and wisdom not leave you, and all of natures power be at your side. It is time young Seth." Announced Kira.

Seth bowed respectfully then turned and walked away. As he followed the path towards the caverns leading out, he glanced back at his fellow villagers, across the crystal clear lake he played in as a boy. He wondered when he would make it back to enjoy it again, but then his thoughts interrupted by some children giggling at his new clothes. He waved and moved on. His good friend Lemule joined him for a bit to bid him farewell.

"Seth, I wish I was going with you, I've heard such stories of these people with their odd ways and contraptions they rely on. You must tell us of your adventures and findings when you return."

"Don't worry my dear friend Lemule," he said amusingly, "...we will share many stories on my return...health and wisdom to you friend."

"And to you Seth, I must stop here now and let you go on, good bye friend." With that, Seth disappeared into the darkness of the cavern.

The entrance was nearly overgrown with lush vines and fragrant bushes, had it not been for the slight breeze gently fanning the leaves he would have passed right by. Although their subterranean village flourished with all kinds of plant life from around the globe, they rarely experienced wind, so the movement caught his attention. Inside it was rather dark; Seth could barely make out his path and the glimmering trails of water seeping through the walls.

In the distance, the sound of a stream cascading over rocks was the only noise aside from his pounding heart. After walking for nearly an hour, the path became narrower and then abruptly stopped at the edge of a great fissure. Had I missed an opening? He wondered. How am I going to cross? There was enough light to see that the path did continue on the other side, but how to get across? It was far too wide to jump, the walls too steep and wet to cling to. He continued looking for another way when he spotted a rope draped along the side hidden by some rocks. As he pulled on it he realized that it raised a rope bridge that traversed the crevasse, securing it tightly he cautiously made his way to the first rung of the walkway. The leather soles of his sandals slipped on the wet, mossy rope as he tested his weight on the bridge, raising his attention level even higher. Slowly, and methodically, Seth made his way over the seemingly bottomless ravine. The adrenaline surged through his body as the bridge swayed under his feet until he reached the other side.

He must be getting closer to the opening, he thought. The noise of falling water was increasing with ever step, the Elders had told him that when he reached the wall of water, he would be on the surface, a world he could never totally understand but dreamt of many times.

The granite hallway was becoming brighter as light somehow was filtering in. Symbols and references to the Akashic writings were etched into the walls. He had seen these before, back at his village in the temple, some he knew, others only Elders of the highest Order were allowed to understand. Those writings were sacred and only taught at certain Mystery Schools. He hoped to be elected to study at them upon his return. Only a few ever were allowed to study the more sacred levels, this journey might make him a better candidate. Some, however, felt that his soul might be stained, unworthy after spending time with the <u>moderns</u>.

The air became wetter with mist as the thundering sound of falling water echoed around him. Turning the corner, Seth stared at the only thing between the fascinating stories he heard as a child and the place he knew as home. Vivid memories flooded his mind's eye; his family, the Elders and the Temples, all the studying he did to help him survive in this <u>over-civilized </u>world. Was he ready? Could he survive long enough to find the one he was sent to look for? It didn't matter; he had to be ready. The Elders had chosen him over all the other students. With that in mind, he closed his eyes, held his breath and stepped through the wall of water.

Instantly, Seth sensed a great warmth he had never felt before; sunlight. Because the village was hidden under a mountain, light was produced by large bells carved out of perfect crystal. When struck they vibrated at the same frequency as visible light. Other bells of varying size and thickness were used regularly for a myriad of tasks ranging from heat production, medicinal purposes, moving large objects and even transportation. The great ancestors had brought this ancient technology when they settled into this region. All members of his kind understood that all things in nature had a harmonic equivalent that could be harnessed for their use. The <u>moderns</u> moved away from nature's power and tried to duplicate it by mechanized means. They thought they could advance civilization, bypassing nature's own designs. This was another thing Seth just couldn't understand. How could anyone ignore nature's gifts? Working with nature was...well, natural. They called it magic; because they forgot how to work <u>with</u> the power of nature, they could not control it.

"And they consider themselves an advanced civilization." Seth mused.

Slowly he opened his eyes, nearly afraid of what he may see, to his amazement he saw nothing but tall pine trees towering over his head, swaying gently back and forth. This wasn't what he expected at all. Where were the crowds, the dwellings? Only trees and the stream, as far as he could see. He knew that it would take the rest of the afternoon to make the trek to the nearest town so taking time to eat something now made sense. In his bag that had been prepared for him, he found lots of fruit and small pieces of cured meat, no telling what or when the next meals may be so Seth mindfully saved some for later.

Following the general path that he had memorized months earlier, hugging the base of the mountain heading northwest, then south; he couldn't help but think of his fellow villagers hundreds of feet below his footsteps.

Then, as he descended from a craggy ledge, a view that took away his breath. He saw a spectacular golden valley, glistening in the distance. There must have been thousands of lights winking at him in the evening dusk.

"I must sleep here for tonight and venture into the town when it is light," he thought. Better for observing as well as not causing alarm by sneaking around in the dark.

Finding a nice little barrier of boulders, Seth laid down beside them, his head on his knapsack he drifted off to sleep rather quickly. In the morning he would be walking right into a new world.

Chapter 3

Mya's head was reeling with curiosity as well as a touch of fear. She turned to Allison and told her she wanted to go home, she wasn't feeling too good, maybe it was the martinis. Allison tried to convince her to finish the tour, there was much left to see of the exhibit, but Mya said she needed to go home and lay down now. Becoming a bit concerned, she agreed to take her friend home. As they pulled up to the apartment, Allison asked.

"Are you okay?"

"I'm fine thanks, I think the cocktails went to my head, that's all. Besides, I have that big presentation to give in the morning."

"Mya..." Allison said in a concerned tone, "would you like me to stay with you tonight? You don't seem yourself."

Leaning over , she gave her friend a tight hug and a kiss on the cheek to thank her for her concern.

"You're such a sweetheart...but you worry too

much...I'll be fine. Drive carefully, I'll call you tomorrow." Waving goodbye, Mya disappeared into her home.

She went straight to the bathroom to wash her face with cold water. Looking up at the mirror, with cool streams of water dripping off her chin, she wondered to herself. What's going on? She had never experienced a phase this strong. Was this even related to a phase or was she really ill? Did she imagine all those things at the museum?

Attempting to take her mind off of it she grabbed the TV remote to try and find some lame infomercial or re-run, but instead only got snow on the screen. Changing channels she realized she wasn't getting anything. Did I totally space out paying my cable bill? Terrific, she thought, what a way to end the day, guess the stereo will have to do. Turning the power on, the sound she heard went straight to her bones...nothing but static on every station!

Slightly panicked she reached for her cordless phone, same results, no dial tone but plenty of static, her cell phone? Nothing. OK...now what? Searching through the medicine cabinet, she found an old prescription for a sleep aid. Taking two, she took off her clothes and crawled into bed trying to make some sense all of this.

Barely hearing the alarm, Mya glanced at the clock and realized it had been going for nearly ten minutes. Stretching and yawning, she couldn't believe how well she had slept, how energetic she felt. No effects from last night, though she could still feel the vibrations coursing through her body.

Jumping into the shower, all of her thoughts focused on her presentation, if she could close this deal it would be the biggest in the history of her company. As the stream of hot water cascaded through her long red hair and over her shoulders, Mya mentally recited the history of her prospects company.

Visualizing their reactions and eagerness to do business with her. She was a great strategist when it came to sales, like a champion chess player, Mya almost always won, today would prove no different.

Strutting out of the conference room with the confidence of a General after a victorious battle, Mya had just sold a 20 million-dollar deal for the interior design of huge casino in the Mediterranean. It was almost becoming too easy, as if everything she asked for, they enthusiastically agreed to. She led all four members of the board along a rosy path with hardly a question from anyone. She had total control over them, what a powerful feeling she thought. But how? Her sketches were hardly studied, the numbers only briefly reviewed, her second and third proposals weren't even offered. They practically closed the deal within forty minutes. With this big of a project anyone would have expected several hours of scrutiny at the least. Mya was tempted to analyze what was going on, but that would wait, it was time to celebrate.

"Mya! ... Mya!" Someone was trying yell over the thumping music and rhythmic swaying of people dancing. Pushing his way through the undulating crowd, it was Martin Jackson, founding partner and Mya's boss, from Jackson, Howard and Vail, Interior Design, LTD. Getting down on both knees, bowing in front of her, Martin kissed Mya's feet exclaiming.

"You're a goddess! How do you do it? You are amazing!"

With that he stood up, gave her one of his expensive cigars and picked her up like a bride, carrying her back to the table with the other designers and sales staff. Everyone was cheering and laughing and praising Mya, there was no doubt who the star was at this party. At one point, Martin climbed onto a chair, barely maintaining balance, raised his glass of bourbon and his voice.

"It's no secret, that without the talent, style, and vision that this young lady has brought to this company, we would not be designing in the international community. This one project is three times larger than anything Jackson, Howard, and Vail has ever done; and she did it single handily. We all owe her a great deal of gratitude. Congratulations, Mya. I only have one question; what's your secret?"

Standing slowly, taking the thick cigar from her mouth.

"OK Martin, here's the secret. After I have shown all my ideas and sketches... I start with this button.." Staring Martin right in the eyes, Mya unbuttons the top button of her suit jacket. The crowd fell silently stunned.

"Then I give them the numbers, how much it will cost and before they have a chance to reply... I move to this button, and then..."

Her fingers undoing the next button. Martin's jaw almost hit the ground from shock, before a naughty smile swept over Mya's lips giving away the joke. The crowd burst into laughter at Martin's gullibility.

"Jeez Mya. Are you trying to give me a heart attack?" She just gave him a sassy smile and blew him a kiss. She loved to tease, and was a master at it.

A few days had passed since the party, Martin told her to take a week off and relax, giving her the keys to his condo in the mountains. It would be wonderful to get away; she needed the break. There something about the mountains that calmed her, something she connected to, even though she grew up in the city.

As soon as she walked in her apartment, the phone rang. It quickly dawned on her that this was the first time it had worked since the museum incident. But when she picked it up it instantly when dead.

"Damn it" she thought. Looking at the caller ID box,

she copied down the number that had just called; it wasn't familiar, an area code somewhere in northern California. Scrolling backwards, the same number appeared three times on caller ID, yet no one had left any messages. A little frustrated, but not too upset, Mya decided to make some hot tea to drink while going through the mail that had piled up while she was away. Dipping the bag in and out of the hot water, Mya leaned over the cup to breathe in the sweet aroma of cinnamon and apples. It reminded her of the cobbler her Grandmother made when she was a child. Her mind drifted, trying to remember what she could of her parents and grandparents, unfortunately there wasn't much.

Her Grandfather passed away when she was an infant, she heard that he was a peculiar man, very tall and a world traveler. She had only seen one old photo of him taken in the mountains. Her Grandmother died when she was nine. Mya was raised, almost solely, by her mom, her father left home when she was thirteen. She remembered him as a strong and ethical man that always tried to make her laugh. His hands were amazingly gentle considering their size and roughness. He had always been kind to her and very stable until about a year before he left. She recalled how restless he had become after he was laid off. There were times she heard her father weeping alone in the study murmuring about not fitting in or something like that. It bothered her because 'Daddies aren't supposed to cry'. She now wished that she had gone in and hugged him, thinking that somehow that may have helped.

When he left, her schoolmates rumored that he had gone crazy and ran into the mountains; kids can be so cruel sometimes, she thought. They were partially right though; her Mom told her that her father had gone to be with nature, where he belonged. They found his body a year after he left, in the backcountry of northwestern Nevada, he died from exposure. All he had with him was his billfold with his ID, a photo of his wife and Mya, and a map of California. Why he was headed there was a mystery. Even though her father had left with no warning, her Mom was never bitter. She never spoke ill of her husband and only said kind things about him to her daughter, though never talking too much about him. The only things she had of his were in a safety deposit box that her mother had left her when she passed away. She had only looked in the box once, and hadn't really had any interest at that time. There were some papers, a few pictures, a book she thought, a pendant and a leather pouch with some rocks in it. He was a bit of a rock hound as she recalled.

Mya's emerald green eyes were puddling with tears when suddenly the phone rang again, snapping her out of her daydream. The tea almost spilled as she raced to the caller ID box, her heart began pounding and she broke out into a sweat when she saw it was the same number from before. If she tried to pick up the phone she knew it would kill the call... but who was trying to reach her from California? Instead of hanging up, this time the caller was leaving a message, it was an older man with a very calm and soothing voice, though unfamiliar.

"Hello Mya... my name is Sinjin, I'm sorry I haven't been able to reach you, but I will try another time. I hope you are feeling better. I think I can help you. Bye for now."

"Who the hell is Sinjin? How does he know that I'm not feeling well?" she thought. Was she going crazy now? Mya wasn't scared by the call, as most people might be, she was determined. Determined to find out who this guy was, what was going on with her body, why all of these electronic devices were going haywire around her? There was only one person she could turn to, one person she could trust to help her unconditionally. It was time to tell Allison...everything.

Chapter 4

Seth woke to the warmth of the early sun striking his face as rays filtered through the tall pine trees. He was anxious to get to the small town and find the elder that was waiting for him. An elder that had left the village many years ago to live among, and study the people that lived on the surface. He was a sort of liaison, a very wise old man called... Sinjin.

You could see the excitement in his eyes as he leapt to his feet, like a child heading for Disneyland, he almost forgot his Morning Prayer. Ever so humbly, Seth knelt down, raising his eyes skyward; he scooped two handfuls of cool soil, stretched his arms out and began giving thanks to his Creator.

"Oh Mighty One, Creator of all blessings and Architect of Nature. I Seth, kneel here before you, to thank you for the honor to be on this journey. I humbly ask for your guidance, protection and wisdom, and that nature's precious power will never leave me. Grant me the courage to use the wonders of the cosmos with respect to my ancestors. Amen."

His people never forgot, or took for granted where they came from or who blessed them, unlike too many other cultures. Letting the soil pour from his hands back to the earth where it came from, Seth grasped the amulet the High Priestess hung around his neck. Focusing on it, he caused it to hum and vibrate until it glowed. It was now in tune with his own harmonics.

Pulling an apple from his knapsack, he headed down the mountain. Walking with full confidence as if he had made the trek a hundred times. He had no map, but he knew exactly where he was going. The village Elders had given him detailed directions to Sinjin's dwelling in town. He had memorized every step. An incredible task for most anyone. But it was nothing extraordinary to him or any of his people. Their entire culture and existence was based on memory. They were incredibly advanced in this area. They never committed anything about their race or culture to paper, helping maintain their secret civilization. The Ancient Ones believed that ones enemies could take away what you committed to paper, or change it to use it against you. But they could never take away what was committed to your mind and soul.

Some people were selected to learn writing and reading for specific reasons, Seth was one of the chosen ones. He needed to be able to survive with little notice where he was going.

Walking over boulders and under branches, he finally made it to the trail he had been looking for. After hiking for over two hours, he was still awestruck at the towering pine trees that dwarfed him. Spying a small stream, he went over to wash his face and take a drink. As he cradled the cool water below his lips, a voice from behind startled him.

"Good morning! How's the water?"

Two young women were hiking up the trail right towards him. They were the first people he had seen since he came to the surface.

"Refreshing." He nervously replied. Was that an appropriate response? He wondered. As they got closer he studied them; they didn't look evil or threatening. In fact he rather liked the way they looked. Young women from his village didn't dress like this. They wore short pants, boots on their feet, and tight fitting T-shirts. They also carried large packs on their backs. They must be going on an adventure too; he thought.

"Are you going up or coming down?" The one with gold hair asked.

"I am headed for the town."

"Ohhh...too bad. We could use the added company." Both of them smiled teasingly as they passed him.

"Maybe next time...bye!" waving as they continued up the trail.

"Umm...bye." That wasn't so bad, smiling from ear to ear. I must press on; Sinjin is expecting me.

Smoke was lazily drifting from the stone chimney of the small cabin. The warm lights from inside comforted and invited Seth. Just as he stepped onto the covered porch, the heavy door opened, but instead of the old man he had expected, was a beautiful young woman. She was probably in her early thirties, long coal black hair that reached about a foot below her waist. Her skin was a light brown and flawless, she had wide brown eyes that mesmerized him. He thought he had reached the wrong dwelling when she spoke.

"Welcome Seth... we have been expecting you, come in. Sinjin is sitting by the fire."

Taking his hat off, he walked in. This dwelling felt almost like home to him, the smells, the warmth, the vibration, all were familiar. He could see the old one sitting in a tall leather chair, gazing into the fire.

"Sinjin?" Seth spoke quietly, wondering if he was interrupting a prayer or meditation.

"Welcome Seth...I trust your journey was pleasant?"

"Yes it was delightful!"

As the Elder stood up Seth bowed his head in reverence. Not only was it customary, but Seth knew of Sinjin's high position of the Order. He had heard many stories of him and of his great journeys.

"I am honored by your generosity Sinjin. Kira and the other Elders send their greetings, as does the entire village."

Sinjin placed his hand on Seth's head signaling him that he may look up now. As he looked up at the man he had heard so much about, he saw a nearly frail old man with deep wrinkles that only an extraordinary life could carve. His hair was white and whispy, his eyes, light blue like aquamarine stones. He wore a familiar brimless cap and traditional long robe. The crystal capped staff seemed to be used more for support than as a symbol of status and power. Then again, Sinjin was well over one hundred and twenty years old; living on the surface seemed to take its toll as well.

"I see you have met Shastina, she is my companion. Shastina is a Native American, from a local tribe, she has been with me many years."

He had been taught about the Native Americans, they had similar believes and were connected to nature much like his own culture.

"Oh... and this is our other companion..." pointing to a dog basking in the glow of the flames, "...Rolex. He's a watch dog."

Seth didn't get the humor, he looked at Shastina as she

rolled her eyes, she'd heard that tired joke too many times.

"You must be hungry after your journey. Shastina... please bring our guest something to eat."

Seth didn't want to eat in front of his hosts, but he couldn't resist. A steaming bowl of stew with warm bread and honey was just what he needed.

When he was done Sinjin asked Shastina to show him to his room. Tomorrow they would begin Seth's final training for the next part of his journey. There was much to learn.

Chapter 5

Mya could hear the shower running when she let herself into Allison's apartment. She waited in the living room for her to come out, pouring herself a drink, thinking of how to tell her best friend about her lifelong secret.

"Allison..." Mya shouted when the shower stopped. She didn't want her friend to be startled as she walked out.

"It's Mya...I let myself in."

"Mya? What are you doing here? Is something wrong? Are you okay?"

Allison rushed into the living room, dripping wet, holding a towel in front of her.

"I'm fine...I think. But I need to talk with you. Go get something on, I'll fix you a drink."

Allison rushed to her room, pulled on an extra big T-shirt and raced back to Mya. Giving her a tight, comforting hug. With a concerned, motherly tone, Allison asked.

"What happened? Is it a guy? Is that creep from your

office bugging you again? Say the word and I'll kick his scrawny little ass!"

Mya laughed at her friends' protectiveness.

"No, nothing like that. There is something about me that I've never told you, and I need to tell you now."

Allison sat back on the couch, pulling her still damp legs under her. She was surprised and a bit bothered. She thought she knew everything about Mya, they had trusted each other for years. What deep, dark secret was in her past? To illustrate her situation, Mya told Allison to turn on her stereo. When she did, there was nothing but static. She tried changing stations, but to no avail.

"You broke my stereo? That's the big secret?"

"No, watch." Mya explained.

Mya walked over to the TV and turned it on. Nothing but static. Now Allison was really confused.

"Okay, now watch the TV and stereo as I leave the room."

Just as she predicted, everything cleared up as she walked out the door, and then went crazy as she returned.

"I can't use the phone either. That's why I haven't called you lately."

"What's causing it? When did it start? This never happened when you have been over before." Asked a confused Allison.

"Well, weird things began happening around me ever since high school. I have these, well, phases that come and go. But it has never been this strong or weird. I'm not sure what to do and you are the only one I can trust to help me."

"Oh sweetie." Allison scooted close to hug her.

"Are you in pain? Is there something I can get to make you feel better? What have the doctors said?"

"I'm not in any pain. Actually I feel great, unusually great. I haven't seen any doctors. You're the only one that knows."

Allison was not only worried for her best friend, but also very curious from a medical standpoint. She had studied pre-med. in college, though did not become a doctor.

"What can I do to help?" Allison asked.

"Well first, I must go back to the exhibit at the museum and finish the tour. I want to see if anything else happens."

"Mya, that exhibit closed two days ago."

"We have to find out where it went to, I have to see it again." Insisted Mya.

"In the mean time, Allison, I need your help to find someone named Sinjin."

"Who's Sinjin?"

"He has called my house a couple of times while I was out, but never left a message. Then he called today and left a strange message. Somehow he knows that something is happening to me and said he can help!"

"Do you know him?" Asked a very concerned Allison.

"No, I've never heard of him. All I know is that he was calling from a town in Northern California. I have his number, but I can't use a phone to call him."

"You want me to call him for you?" Offered Allison.

"Yes, I'll give you a list of questions, but I want you to tape the conversation so I can hear his voice and demeanor."

"Excuse me...isn't it illegal to record a conversation without the other party knowing?"

"Apparently not for <u>everyone</u> in the country." Mya smirked.

"Do you want to come back to my place and work out a plan? Or we could start tomorrow, Saturday."

"I was just going to read and go to bed early, but I'd rather go with you. Let me grab a few things." Responded

Allison, as she jumped up from the couch.

Mya and Allison stayed up most of the night scripting the call Allison would make. Talking about what they suspected was going on, and some experiences Mya had when she was younger. Two-thirty in the morning came quickly, so they decided to go to bed and make the call in the morning.

Mya woke to the smell of brewing coffee and Belgian waffles cooking in the kitchen. Allison had been up a couple of hours already and wanted to surprise her friend with breakfast, she had just finished making her plate when Mya walked in and asked her what she was up to.

"We have a big day ahead of us and we need a good start. Sit down. Do you want sour cream with your peaches and waffles?"

"No thanks, unlike you, I have to work at my figure." Quipped Mya.

Allison seemed to be able to eat anything without any consequences; Mya liked to tease her about it regularly.

"So, what's the big day consist of?" Asked Mya.

"Well, for starters, we are going to see a friend of mine, Simon Robertson. He's a doctor."

"Woah! I said no one is to know but you." Mya interrupted quickly.

"Don't worry, I haven't told him anything. Besides, I went on a few dates with him in college; he owes me a few favors. I'm going to have him run a few tests for us. We have to know a few things before we call Mr. Sinjin. I told Simon this must be done without any other help. Totally confidential."

Mya was very concerned about any involvement of doctors. She had kept her secret several years and didn't want anyone else to know until she had a grip on what was happening.

"Oh, by the way, I found out that the exhibit we saw has moved on to Santa Cruz, California."

Mya's eyes lit up. What was in Santa Cruz? That name seemed very familiar, but she did not remember why? She had never been there; she had never been north of Santa Barbara.

"Can you get a few days off to go with me?"

"I don't know Mya. When? I have a big project coming up."

"As soon as possible. Oh Allison...I need you with me."

Allison knew she couldn't let her best friend down. But she also knew her boss would have a fit. Oh well, she thought. You can have lots of bosses and jobs in your life, but a best friend lasts a lifetime. Besides, she knew Mya would drop anything in a second to help her. When she agreed, she could see tears in Mya's eyes as she thanked her. This obviously was extremely important to her.

Mya's hands were sweating and nearly shaking as she was introduced to Dr. Robertson.

"Allison, this is really unusual, you haven't told me any of her symptoms, or even what we're looking for."

"Don't worry Simon, I'll read the results myself. I told you, this was very confidential."

Allison flirted with him to get him to drop his worry. She was an expert at that. Mya couldn't help but notice how she turned him into a dopey kid with her manipulations.

"Okay, lets start with an MRI."

Escorting Mya to the table, he instructed her to lie still for the duration. As Dr. Robertson settled at the console behind the glass that separated the equipment from them, he reassured Mya that the process was painless. Toggling switches and turning knobs to begin the scan, he waited for the prompts on the screen to allow him to put in her data. Surprisingly, the monitor remained blank. Not responding.

"I told you, I need a technician to operate this stuff. I must have forgotten something." Explained Simon.

Allison knew differently, it was Mya causing the disruption, not Simon's lack of expertise on the equipment.

"Okay Simon, let's do a full blood screen to start. After that, I have an idea."

Once the three tubes of blood had been drawn, Allison suggested that they perform an electroencephalogram, to monitor her brainwave patterns. They set her up in the x-ray room; there was plenty of lead protection between Mya and the monitoring room. Allison hoped it would prevent any disruption from Mya to the equipment.

Once they secured the electrodes to her scalp, they returned to the monitor and turned it on. This time it was working. Simon was confused, however, seeing unusual patterns in areas where there was normally no activity, hers was erratic and nearly off the chart. He assumed he had something set up incorrectly. Allison convinced him to let the readings continue. Studying them, they noticed that nearly all of the waves were sub-normal. They registered far below any normal activity, yet her Alpha waves were pegged out of range. Allison tore off the graph paper and shoved it in her shoulder bag, not allowing Simon to study too much of it.

"Simon, can you get me several lead aprons?" Asked Allison.

"Sure...why?"

"I have an idea. Meet us back at the MRI exam room."

Once there, they placed the lead aprons on the backside of the monitoring equipment. Allison was hoping that whatever disruption was being generated by Mya, would be blocked by the aprons.

"Simon, have her lay on the bed while you run a system test."

"Okay, but you won't get any readings with the magnets turned off." The confused doctor answered. Dr. Robertson ran through the checklist to perform the system test. Everything was operating fine, when he noticed that the monitor was forming an outline of Mya's body, and then began filling in detail. But how was it getting any data with the magnets off? He wondered. Simon was confused; Allison was not.

"Print out a color copy and then delete the data. Next, turn on the system and run a regular test."

Simon did as requested. As the results of the test were coming up on screen, he noticed they looked just like the results from before.

"Now print out a color copy of the second test, mark it, and delete these files also. Now, let's go to the lab, get the blood test results and go home." Ordered Allison.

Mya sipped her Merlot nervously as her friend compared the results with her old medical books. Allison couldn't find anything that resembled what she was seeing in the MRI. It looked like waves of descending intensity radiating from specific points on her body. Seven points to be exact, the largest being located near the solar plexus. Eastern medicine called it the 'heart chakra'. She had read a little bit about eastern medicine and philosophy in college, but didn't remember much detail. At any rate, Mya was obviously generating some type of energy from these seven points on her body. Allison looked over at her friend who was now curled up and asleep on her couch. She couldn't help but wonder what she must be dreaming about.

They had decided to drive to Santa Cruz the next day, to catch the 'Lost Memories in Time' exhibit again before it closed for good. Mya also decided to hold off on calling Sinjin until she and Allison had checked out a few things at the exhibit. They would call from California.

Chapter 6

Everyone had gone to bed, but Seth couldn't sleep. He should be exhausted from the long day of travelling; yet he was wide-awake. He sat near the open window of his room, gazing in amazement at the vast night sky. There were so many stars, so many other worlds that he had heard about. Back home in his village, there are a few holes in the upper surface where you could see the stars. They were near the Temples, but you could only see a small portion of the sky. Here, he could see everything, it was breathtaking. He envisioned what it was like for his ancestors and the Travelers that used the stars to guide their great sea and airships from their homeland so long ago. The different formations looked familiar to him. They looked like some of the drawings on the ceilings of the Great Temples. The night sky was filled with the wonderful aroma of pine and sage, it was nearly intoxicating, helping him drift off to sleep.

Seth's eyes fluttered open to the sound of a mother raccoon and her baby, rustling through a nearby bush looking for breakfast. The mountain sky was brightening as the sun prepared to break over the horizon. He quickly went to peer out the hallway to see if he had overslept, he didn't want someone of Sinjin's stature to think him lazy. Fortunately, no one had risen yet, though when he turned his head to look the other way, he was greeted by Rolex, who was sitting by his door. Startled at first, Seth relaxed when the big dog gave him a sloppy, wet kiss on his hand.

After breakfast, Sinjin and Seth headed into the woods for a walk. It seemed like an eternity of silence before the Elder spoke.

"Seth...I know that you were chosen for this journey from many students, and that you have studied very hard. But there are many things about the surface people and machines they depend on, that you have not been taught. In order to blend in with them, you must not act too surprised by them."

Seth could not imagine what he had not heard about. He knew that these people had land ships and air ships to travel great distances. He had learned about devices that let them see and communicate with others far away.

"Sinjin, why do these people depend on these machines?"

"They have forgotten how to use their own energy and spirit. Laziness has blinded them to their own powers. Many civilizations have convinced themselves that they can do better than Nature. They are foolish."

The Elder explained. Seth nodded his head in agreement.

"Are all people on the surface evil and greedy?" Asked Seth.

"Not all actually, most have good souls, but their societies are confused and too pre-occupied with money." Explained Sinjin.

Seth was somewhat relieved, but still concerned about these machines.

"Should I avoid these devices?"

"Do you see this amulet around my neck? It is just like yours. You must never remove it from your neck while on the surface. If you don't have it on, your own energy will interfere and overpower their devices, keeping them from working. Someone will notice."

"Is our life energy stronger than theirs?"

Asked Seth.

"No, they have only forgotten how to focus and use it. And that is part of your task Seth, to teach one who is unaware but needs to learn of her power. To help her learn our ways, she is one of our kind and does not know of her ancestry."

"How am I to find her?"

Seth didn't know he had to locate someone he did not know, in a world he had never lived in.

"She is on her way to California now, you will find her a town south of here. I will tell you later where she will be. You must use your mind so she can find you."

Seth was not told of the importance of this woman, but he could tell from Sinjin's demeanor that he must not fail.

"When shall I leave to find her?" He asked.

"Tomorrow."

Although he was anxious, tomorrow seemed too soon. There was still much he didn't know about these people.

"In the morning, Shastina will take you to the place you will meet the woman at. I'm certain you will enjoy your first trip in a truck."

Seth could barely contain his excitement; he had seen images of trucks and cars before. He never thought he would be able to ride in one.

As they concluded their walk, the old man faced him and placed his frail hands on Seth's shoulders. Looking into Sinjin's light blue eyes, he could feel the incredible energy and wisdom as his spoke.

"All of our ancestors will guide you, embrace your alliance with Natures energy. Do not be blinded by the other's confusion and denial. Trust yourself, trust and rely on the ancient teachings. When you find this woman, bring her back here. You must not force her, she must come of her own will."

"I do not know what she looks like, what do her people call her?"

Seth asked.

Sinjin's eye's glanced at the ground for a moment, as he turned to walk back to the cabin he said.

"Her name is Mya."

Seth had heard that name before, but couldn't recall where. He decided not to ask anymore questions about her. Sinjin walked back to the cabin by himself.

Chapter 7

Allison had noticed that Mya was getting more and more anxious as they got closer to their hotel in Santa Cruz. They had been taking turns driving since leaving home yesterday, the trip seemed to have taken some stress from Mya. Both had been laughing a lot, singing and flirting with passing truckers. But ever since they had crossed into California, Mya began to get quieter. Neither had spoken about the exhibit or Sinjin, both were taking a 'wait and see what happens' approach.

As they pulled into the hotel driveway, the valet greeted them. When he reached for her door, Allison leaned over and whispered in Mya's ear.

"I wonder if he's on the room service menu?"

They both giggled out loud like teenagers.

Once in their room, they decided to unwind for the rest of the day, tomorrow they would find the exhibit.

The warm pacific breeze carried the smell of the fish

market up to their balcony, just as it carried the gulls on their search for food scraps. With the glow of the sun melting into the watery horizon, Mya questioned her own sanity.

"Allison, do you think I'm losing it? Am I going to end up like my father?"

"Mya, you're the most sane person I know."

"Than how can I explain why I'm here? Why I've dragged my best friend here?"

Asked Mya. Of course Allison didn't have the answer either, all she could do was be there for her.

"Maybe we'll find out tomorrow."

After the brilliant light show of the sunset had disappeared, Mya went back inside and pulled out a box she had brought along and stuffed in her backpack. Allison had seen the box, but respectfully didn't mention it, assuming it was private. Mya stared at it, trying to decide if she should open it. It was the safety deposit box with her father's belongings in it. She wondered if there was anything inside that might shed some light on what was going on with her. Maybe some medical records.

Noticing that Allison had gone to bed, Mya carefully turned the key in the lock, and slowly opened the lid. Until now, she had always felt indifferent about the contents; maybe subconsciously she was afraid of what she may find. Maybe her childhood anger towards her father would resurface.

Peering inside, there were a couple of hand drawn maps, two leather bound books and some loose rocks. Also, what looked like a container made of petrified wood. Lying under the maps were a leather pouch and a silk pouch. Inside the silk pouch were a pendant and some pictures, one of her mother as a young adult and another of Mya as a child, with her father. The other photos were of landscapes with no people in them. As she looked at the photo of her dad and her, she started to cry.

"What made you leave us?"

Mya silently asked her father. As she stared at the handsome man she barely remembered, she questioned his motives for leaving. Had he gone crazy like the school kids said? Was he fleeing from something? Or fleeing to something? Would she ever find out, and did she really want to know? Setting the picture aside, she wiped away the tears from her cheeks and slipped her father's pendant over her head. It was a stone with a faint carving around it and suspended from a leather strap. Not something she would buy, but thought it might make her feel closer to her father.

Mya looked into the leather pouch and only found more rocks. The maps were of North America, South America, Egypt, Asia and Antarctica. There was also a map of California and what looked like a map of the Constellations. All of them were hand drawn with X's and V's and odd symbols, dotted throughout. Probably geological sites, places he had dug for rocks or wanted to. The old books however, were strange. They too were handwritten, no dates or author, but the writing was in the same hand as person that drew the maps. What really threw her, was the language, she didn't recognize it. She was too tired to figure it out; so she put everything back in the box, except the picture of her dad, and the pendant she had on, and then slipped it back into her backpack. Crawling under the warm blankets, she clutched her father's pendant and drifted off to sleep.

Chapter 8

Seth rose early; he was so excited he had barely slept the night before. As the horizon began to lighten, his anticipation grew, he wished he could force the sun to rise faster. Soon enough he heard someone in the other room, it was Shastina preparing the breakfast meal and starting a fire in the fireplace.

"Good morning."

He said as he entered the room to help with the firewood.

"Good morning to you." She answered.

"Are you ready for your trip?" She asked with a smile.

"Yes! I am anxious to see the city. Have you been there?"

"Not to that city, but others like it. We will stop in the small town that is down the road first to pick up some items for you." She said.

After a few minutes Seth realized he had not seen Sinjin yet and asked where he was.

"He is in his room meditating and will not be done until the sun has set again."

"I will not see Sinjin before I leave?" He asked.

"No, but he has given me everything you need."

Shastina walked over to a cabinet and handed him an envelope. Inside were some papers with prayers and blessings written on them, a map showing the stars along with several hundred dollars. She noticed the slightly confused look on his face.

"You have learned about their money haven't you?"

"Yes, I wasn't sure that I would be exchanging it with them though."

"I'll give you a refresher course during our drive."

Seth felt relieved; he didn't want to appear ignorant to her, although this was one area of their culture he didn't fully understand.

After finishing his breakfast, Shastina told him to get his knapsack; it was time to go. He followed her outside to a small building and helped her open the large double doors. Inside he saw an old pick up truck half covered with a canvas. As Shastina pulled away the canvas, Seth's eyes widened, it was marvelous.

"Is this an automobile?" he asked, with the enthusiasm of a child. Shastina nodded as she climbed in. Seth walked up to the passenger door; she motioned him that it was okay for him to get in. He saw the door handle and gave it a pull, but the door didn't open.

"You have to push the button first, and then pull."

She instructed. Looking at the side of the door he saw a small silver button, pressed it and then pulled the handle. Nothing happened. He tried again; still the door did not open.

"You must push the button and pull on the handle at the same time."

37

She instructed. With a finger from one hand, he pressed the button and grabbed the handle with the other hand. Pushing and pulling until the truck was rocking, he could not open the door. Frustrated, he looked up at Shastina, she got out and came around to help. He showed her what he was doing. She laughed to herself when she saw that he had been pressing the keyhole for the lock instead of the button that was part of the handle. When she opened the door for him he felt a little embarrassed that he couuld not figure out something so simple.

Once inside, she showed him how to use the seat belt and then started the engine. The roar of the engine reminded him of a beast in a cave. With a quick shudder, they were headed off down the dirt road.

He watched in amazement as her feet pushed on pedals and moved a lever that came up from the floor with her hand. It looked very complicated. Shastina looked over to see Seth gripping tightly to the dashboard. His knuckles may have been white, but his smile was ear to ear.

"It will get smoother when we get on the main road." Remarked Shastina.

As they bounced down the dirt road he wondered how safe this machine was, but just as she predicted, the ride soon smoothed out. Suddenly, another vehicle appeared in front of them. It was getting closer and moving right at them. He was getting concerned, was it going to hit them? Seth braced for the impact when the other vehicle raced right next to them, barely avoiding a certain collision. Looking at Shastina, he noticed that she was as calm as ever.

"Why did they try to hit us?" He asked.

"They weren't trying to hit us. They just have to stay on their side of that yellow line." She explained.

It was still dangerously close as far as he was concerned. As they neared town, they encountered more and more vehicles. They were of many different shapes and colors, some had many passengers while others had but one. Seth assumed that each vehicle must be designed for a different purpose.

Finally, Shastina began slowing their vehicle. Seth could see more and more dwellings; they looked very different from his own, quite large. The office buildings and stores reminded him of Temples, because of their size. They were also very close together. Seth had hardly spoken since they had pulled into town; he was mesmerized by all of the people walking around and wondered where they might be going.

"Okay, here we are."

Shastina announced, as she parked the truck in front of a building. She turned the key and the truck's engine went silent, as though the beast's breath had been taken away.

"We're at the market. We need to go inside and buy a few things and then we will continue. I want you to watch me closely, so you will know what to do when you are not with me."

Nervously, he followed her into the store. He couldn't help but stare at everyone and everything.

"Oh" Shastina turned back to remind him. "Keep your hat on all the time."

She didn't want to draw attention to his peculiar forehead.

Seth marveled at all of the packaged items in the general store, the touristy nick-knacks and novelties. Shastina motioned him to stay closer to her so he could learn. She picked up some fruit, a bag of peanuts, a watch and a map for Santa Cruz. As they walked toward the counter, something caught Seth's eye. He looked over at Shastina and said "Home", as he pointed to a small plastic snow globe. Inside was a miniature replica of a snow-capped mountain, at the base in big blue letters it read Mt. Shasta. Shastina smiled and nodded her head.

"Yes...that is home." She took it from the shelf and carried it to the counter with the rest of the items. He watched very closely as the clerk rang up the items and gave her the total. Shastina handed him some paper money; the clerk gave her more paper money back as well as some coins. This was the most confusing part to him. He waited until they got back in the truck to ask her to explain the transaction.

Once back in the vehicle, she put all of the items in his backpack except the watch.

"Hold out your arm. Wear this on your wrist to keep track of time."

"What is time?"

He asked innocently.

"Time is a measurement of a day, and the numbers on the watch are a specific 'time' of that day."

Still confused, he wondered why anyone would need to assign a number to a portion of a day, but he accepted it.

Back on the road, Shastina tried to explain how to use the money Sinjin had given him. He listened intently, but couldn't help but take in the countryside and towns they were speeding past. They only stopped once to get gas, and before long they were approaching their destination. Seth's anxiety began to build.

The city of Santa Cruz was much larger than anything he had imagined; there were so many buildings and vehicles. People were everywhere; they were all scurrying around as if they were in a hurry. It was all so very noisy. After a short time of maneuvering though all of the streets, Shastina pulled the truck into the parking lot of a small motel.

"This is where you will be staying until you find Mya

and return to Sinjin. I'll go in and get your key."

After she returned, they went to his room, it was modest but comfortable.

"Shastina, why is there a lock on the door?"

Asked a concerned Seth.

"Am I being imprisoned here?"

"No, it is to keep other people out, not to keep you in." She explained.

"Will I find Mya here?" He asked.

"No, you must meditate and use your mind and energy to locate her, just as you were taught by Sinjin. Once you have found her, you must find your way back to us on your own. I will not be back to pick you up."

"I understand. I will start my prayers and meditation immediately."

Responded Seth.

"I must leave now, remember all that you have been taught and trust yourself and your ancestors to guide you. Good bye Seth."

Shastina shut the door behind her. Seth was now truly alone in a world he knew so little about. He was determined not to be afraid, yet there was still some amount of fear in him. Fear of letting Sinjin, and his village down.

After thanking his ancestors and his Creator through prayers, Seth peered out the window to marvel at the city. It was now past sunset, and the street lights had come on. He knew that he should stay in until the morning when it was lighter, but his excitement was too much. Maybe if he ventured out tonight, he could begin learning how to blend in before he found Mya.

Standing in front of a mirror, he reviewed his clothing, did he look like everyone else? Would he draw attention to himself? Recalling what Sinjin had told him, he made sure he still was wearing the pendant given to him at the village, put on his hat and stepped out of his room.

Cars were speeding past him on the street, they fascinated him, yet made him nervous as he thought they may lose control and hit him. Gradually he began walking down the sidewalk, looking in the store windows, his confidence building as he passed other people without anyone staring at him. This place was much louder than he expected, mostly from the automobiles, but a different bunch of sounds were coming from inside one of the buildings up the street.

He stood outside for awhile, observing the people as they went in and out. Many of them in pairs of women and men holding hands, some in small groups. Seth walked closer to the door, the noise was so loud it was nearly intolerable, he hesitated, maybe he should go back to his room. Suddenly he was pushed from behind as a group of people surged through the door. Now he had no choice, he was in.

Looking around the dimly lit room, he saw a large crowd of people in the center of the room jumping up and down, whirling around while holding each other by the hands. Then he realized that the noise that drew him here had a distinct beat. It was music and apparently everyone was dancing to it. They had music and dancing in his village, but it didn't sound anything like this. What he was hearing was nearly hypnotic, and he loved it.

Everyone there seemed to be having so much fun, he moved closer to the rail so he could see the musicians and people dancing. Even though he had not planned on coming inside, he felt it was a good opportunity to study people. It was interesting to see how different everyone's clothing was.

There was a man wearing a silken shirt, that was left unbuttoned nearly to his naval, very tight pants that were black and shiny. Seth figured that he must be wealthy and well known, because he wore many rings on his hands and gold chains around his neck. He also spoke to every woman he passed by. The women dressed very differently than each other. One might be clothed in pants and a coat, another wearing a long dress while some wore skirts that barely covered their rear ends. He liked those the best.

Unexpectedly, a pretty woman came up and asked if he wanted a drink.

"I'm not thirsty, thank you." He replied.

As she walked over to someone else, he thought it would be a good idea to follow her and see how she interacts with other people. Leaning over she handed the two glasses, with pink water in them, to the men sitting together.

"Here are your Cosmopolitans gentlemen. That will be fourteen seventy-five, please." She said.

One of the men replied.

"This one's on me.", and handed her a piece of paper money, "and keep the change Honey".

Seth continued following the waitress until she turned around and said in a rather stern voice.

"If you're not going to order a drink, you better leave before there's trouble".

The last thing he needed was any trouble, so he left the club quickly. As he continued walking through town, looking in all the store windows, he practiced greeting people as they passed by. Not everyone returned greetings the same way, some said hello back, others replied with 'Hi', or 'Good Evening'. Most were polite although some just nodded their heads or ignored his greeting altogether. All in all it was a good learning step and he was gaining confidence with his communication skills. It was getting late and Seth was tiring, so he headed back to his room. Tomorrow he had to find Mya.

Chapter 9

It was still early; the Museum had not opened yet, Seth was eager to go inside, this is where Mya should be. He had been guided to this place by an unseen force, he knew that it was his ancestors and Sinjin that had led him here. He waited across the street in a park. He found a majestic oak tree to sit under. He missed the trees of home, but this was as welcoming as those. Seth took out some bread and nuts from his backpack and shared them with a squirrel and some birds. He felt he more in common with them than he did with the surface people.

Something caught his attention causing him to look up, he saw that people were already entering the museum. Time had passed quickly while he daydreamed with the squirrels.

There were many steps leading up to the entrance, which was surrounded by several tall columns of marble. Obviously this was a place of great importance. As he walked down the long hall, a sign directed him through a door where a man said,

"Come on in, today is a free day".

Seth smiled in return and started making his way through the exhibits.

Many of the displays and artifacts looked familiar and it bothered him a little when they were referred to as 'ancient' or 'primitive'. Seth re-focused his attention to the reason he was there. He knew she was there, he could feel her energy, he only had to follow it. The waves of energy led him to the next floor, to an exhibit displaying various stones, jewelry and artifacts used in ceremonies and rituals. There were a few people mulling around the various displays, but he instinctually knew which one was Mya from the energy she was producing. Seth remained at a distance behind her and her friend, who was locked arm in arm with her as if to protect her.

She was tall, though not as tall as himself, her hair was long and red, a color he had never seen before. Her skin was cinnamon in color, and eyes that melted him. She looked like a goddess. How should he get her attention without frightening her?

Mya was obviously nervous and Allison was concerned for her best friend as they edged closer to the display.

"Are you sure this is the same display you remember Mya?" Asked Allison.

"Yes, it's rearranged a bit differently though".

As they looked around anxiously, Allison let go of her friend's arm to take a closer look at a ceremonial bowl a few feet away. Suddenly, the stone pendant around her neck began to feel warm, not burning, but comforting. Then she heard a soft whisper.

"Mya".

It wasn't Allison's voice; besides, she was too far away.

"Mya, I'm here"

She couldn't tell where it was coming from. It was as if

the voice was surrounding her, no distinct direction. Looking all around, there was nobody close enough to whisper. Then, she saw a young man, probably in his twenties, dressed like a backpacker and wearing a wide brimmed hat, standing about fifty feet away. While looking straight at him she heard her name again, but his lips never moved. She nodded her head, acknowledging him. Sensing that she was not afraid, he slowly approached her.

As he neared, she felt her body tingling and humming like it had before, yet she remained very calm.

"Are you Sinjin?" Asked Mya.

"Oh no...my name is Seth. Sinjin has sent me to find you."

"Well who is he and what does he want?" Demanded Mya.

"Sinjin is one of our most venerated Elders. He wishes to meet with you, to teach you about your ancestry, I am told it is important."

"Can he explain what's going on with my mind lately? Where is he at?"

"I'm certain he can. He lives in a cottage outside the town called Mt. Shasta. He is too frail to travel here, so we must travel to him when you are ready." Explained Seth.

"I'm not going anywhere else until I get some more answers. Allison?"

Mya called for her friend. When she didn't see her, she realized there was nobody else at the exhibit but her and Seth.

"Where is she?" Mya asked in a panic.

"She is still here, everyone is. We are just on another plane for the moment." Explained Seth.

"Another plane? What the hell are you talking about?" Mya was becoming confused and a little irritated by all the riddles.

Seth tried to explain in more detail.

"You and I have moved to a different 'plane' of harmonics. In other words, we are on the same cosmic frequency, which is different than everyone else at this moment. It is a much lower one."

Mya was in disbelief, how could this be.

"Okay...Seth...how exactly did we get to this so called plane?"

"I simply matched our energy and then lowered our harmonics together. It's easy, if you practice enough."

He could see that she still didn't understand, so he continued to explain.

"In your culture, you have a device called a radio to transmit sounds, right?"

"Uh-huh." Mya was trying to make the connection.

"The radio transmitter sends sound over many different frequencies into the cosmos, yet when your device 'tunes' in on only one of those frequencies, you hear only the sounds traveling there. Does that mean that all of the sounds traveling on the thousands of other frequencies are no longer there? Of course not, you simply aren't on the same frequency."

"You know what? This is starting to make way too much sense. And that's what's scaring me!"

Seth was smiling with pride from his explanation.

"All beings can alter their physical and spiritual energies. Your people have just forsaken Natures' gift in exchange for machines."

"Your people?" Mya was slightly offended.

"Who are my people? Aren't they the same as your people? Or are you from Jupiter or something?"

Seth apologized for offending her, he knew it was not her fault. He quickly changed the subject.

"We all have the power of Nature to do wonderful

things, we are all connected to the same energy. Here, watch."

Seth reached in his backpack and pulled out some seeds that he had found by the trees outside.

"Give me your hand."

Placing the seeds in her palm, he closed her soft, manicured hands with his, he could feel that her life energy was vibrant. He didn't say another word, Mya just stared into his eyes, they were so comforting and honest. It was if she could read his soul. Then, her hands began to feel warm, and although her body had not stopped humming since seeing him, it was increasing. Now she could feel something in her hands moving. Seth smiled and said,

"Look what you have done."

Mya opened her hands and was astonished to find that the seeds had sprouted and were flourishing in her palm.

"You see? All you had to do was share your life energy with the seeds, just as you share it with the ones you love."

Something inside was connecting, somehow it was making a little bit of sense; a tear fell down her cheek.

"Where did you learn this?" She asked.

"From the same place you learned to walk, and to love. From those who care about us, parents teachers and our ancestors."

Mya sat quietly for several moments, staring at the new life in her palms. She looked up.

"Where are you from Seth?"

For the next several hours, she sat mesmerized as he told her of his village, his childhood and studies. He told her fascinating stories of the ancestors and other worlds. Most of it was so far fetched it was seemed impossible. But something about Seth made her believe him. She could sense his honesty. She also sensed that he had jaded view of her culture, and something in him wanted to experience her world. Although he didn't admit it, it must have been difficult to spend your entire life in an underground village.

"I need to speak to Allison and I want you to meet her. How do we get back to 'her plane'?"

Just as she finished her question, Mya saw her friend walking toward another display calling her; they were back.

"Allison! Over here." Shouted Mya.

"Where did you go Mya? One minute you're behind me, and the next you're gone."

"I went to talk with someone. Allison, I want you to meet Seth. He knows Sinjin."

Reluctantly, she reached out to shake his hand.

"He does? Okay, where is this creep so I can kick his ass for harassing my best friend."

Allison was always ready to protect her buddy.

"He wasn't harassing me, he was only trying to help me with my problem." Mya interrupted.

"Anyway, I've agreed to go with Seth to Sinjin's to figure out what's going on with me."

"Mya? Can I talk with you…alone!"

Allison grabbed Mya by the arm and pulled her aside. In a stern whisper, Allison voiced her concerns.

"Are you crazy? You don't know this psycho or where he's taking you. He's probably just trying to get into your skirt, or worse."

"Allison, I really believe this guy, it's a gut feeling. You know my gut feelings."

She knew what she meant, when Mya said she had a gut feeling about something, she was always right. That's how she became so successful.

"Besides, I don't think he'd know what to do even if he did find his way into my skirt."

They both started to giggle as they looked back at the tall innocent looking stranger.

Mya finally convinced Allison that she knew what she was doing, and after spending more time with Seth at the museum, she began to trust him as well. They agreed that Allison would take the car back home while Seth and Mya went to meet Sinjin. After she learned what she needed, Mya would catch a plane home. Before they parted though, there was shopping to be done, and the girls decided to treat Seth to a night on the town.

As they drove up and down the shopping district, Seth appreciated the ride from the back seat; this vehicle rode so much smoother than Shastina's truck. In the front, the girls danced and wiggled in their seats to the music coming from the CD player, he thought it looked like they had sat in a pile of red ants. They found a place to park and went into a small boutique called Margie's. Wandering around the store, the girls stroked every article of clothing, commenting on each one.

"Ooh, feel this one Allison!"

"Mya, look at the neckline on this, it's so cute. You should try it on."

Seth just followed along quietly, like an obedient puppy. As they went from store to store, he noticed other 'puppies' being dragged around by the women they were with. What amazed him is why there were so many choices and so many colors of clothing. He assumed there must be a law prohibiting two people from wearing the same dress. Finally after several stores and purchases, they stopped at an ice cream parlor, as it was a warm day.

"Do you like ice cream Seth?" Mya asked.

"What is it? I don't think I have ever had any."

He replied, as he tried to look in the window.

"It's a frozen dessert made from cream and sugar and flavoring." Explained Mya.

"It's a miracle food..." Allison piped in sarcastically,

"...if you're depressed and skinny, it makes you happy and fat."

Mya ordered for Seth since he didn't know any of the flavors, she got him a rich vanilla with caramel swirled in and chunks of chocolate. Cautiously taking a small taste, Seth's eyes lit up and broke into a smile as the mix of flavors hit him. He loved it; so much that it was gone in no time. The girls just laughed, he seemed more like a seven-year-old boy than a man in his twenties. When they finished and the check came, Seth wanted to pay; recalling what he witnessed at the club the previous night; he exclaimed.

"I've got this one." Digging into his envelope with the money Sinjin had given him.

"Here you go, keep the change."

Mya and Allison looked at each other in disbelief; he paid the nine-dollar tab with a one hundred-dollar bill and told the waitress to keep the change. When he saw the puzzled look on everyone's faces, he worried that he hadn't given her enough. The waitress thanked him and quickly exited before he changed his mind. Seth apologized.

"I'm sorry, I still don't understand the money exchange requirements, did I offend her?"

"Hardly," Allison replied, "I think you just made her week."

"How much money do you have in there?"

Mya waived her finger at the dark brown envelope.

Embarrassed for not knowing or even caring, Seth took out a large stack of money and handed it to her.

"I do not know, can you tell me?"

Half scolding him, Mya exclaimed.

"You don't carry this kind of cash around, let alone wave it around for everyone to see!" Scolded Mya.

Mya held the money close to her lap so no one could

see her counting. It was all one hundred- dollar bills, forty-nine of them. Seth explained that Sinjin had given him the money. Allison leaned over and whispered in her friend's ear.

"Either this guy is for real, or just rich and stupid."

The girls thought it might be dangerous for him to walk back to his room with all that cash, so they drove him back instead. Seth sat in the back seat, still marveling at what passed outside his window.

"Allison, I'm going to drop you off at our room first, take Seth to his hotel and talk awhile more; then I'll be back."

Allison was slightly concerned, but knew she didn't stand a chance of changing her mind. Once back at their hotel, Mya told Seth to wait in the car while she went up-stairs to get something. Like a worried mother, Allison in-structed her friend to be home early or to call.

"Don't trust this guy we just met Mya!"

Mya smiled and hugged her long time buddy tightly, assuring her she would be fine.

Seth had moved to the front seat and was touching and studying the car's instruments when Mya returned. After tossing her backpack into the back seat, Mya climbed in.

"Well Seth, you seem to know a bit about me, now tell me more about you and Sinjin."

Although Seth was more interested in learning how to navigate this vehicle than talking about himself, he sat back and began to tell her about his ancestry and homeland; Le-muria. Mya's mind was spinning while listening to tales of a culture and land that seemed impossible. It sounded more like a storybook than fact, but Seth's descriptions and en-thusiasm made her soul want to believe.

Soon they were at Seth's motel. Mya wanted to hear more so she asked if she could come in. She felt a safeness with this stranger that she didn't want to rationalize. His words were penetrating her soul, reaching a place she had protected all of her life. After another hour of Seth's history lesson, Mya interrupted.

"I want to show you something, stay here".

Dashing out to her car, she grabbed her backpack and brought it inside. Laying out her father's items, she asked.

"Can you tell me anything about any of these?"

She didn't know why he might know anything; she had not mentioned her father to him.

Seth looked at the old hand drawn map first, without him saying anything, she could tell he knew something.

"What is it?"

His eyes were wide, scanning the symbols that dotted the map.

"I have seen these markings on the ceiling of our Temple and in the Ancient's writings." He exclaimed. Suddenly he expression turned to concern.

"These are sacred papers, I don't think I should be looking at them. Only Elder's are allowed to read these."

Setting them back on the bed as if they were hot coals, Seth was reluctant to look upon them longer.

"Sinjin must see these, he can read them for you."

Mya was very puzzled by his reaction.

"What about these?"

Seth seemed almost afraid of what else she had. Slowly, a carved box emerged, the one she couldn't open. Seth's eyes lit up quickly as he took it from her. He looked up at her and smiled broadly, then closed his eyes as if to focus on a task. Suddenly the edges of the box slid open, without even the slightest effort.

"It is a 'szja'. When a child comes of age, and has mastered energy control, they are given this box. In it, one places items that are sacred to them. On the bottom of the szja, there is a stone that you must harmonize with to open the sides."

"Is there anything in the box?" Mya asked.

Reaching his long fingers through the opening, he withdrew a tiny picture and a precisely carved stone. Seth thought it was some type of key. As he studied it, he noticed Mya was silent, her eyes began to swell with tears.

"Is something the matter?" Seth asked. She said nothing. He looked at the tiny image in her hand.

"Who is it?"

In a soft quivering voice, Mya mouthed the words,

"It's me"

Silence took over the small room.

Seth took Mya's hands; hers seemed dwarfed in his.

"Who does this belong to?"

"My father" she whispered.

A comforting smile came over Seth's face.

"That means you were the most sacred thing to him."

All of a sudden there was a brilliant flash of blue-white light outside, followed by a tremendous boom of thunder. Seth leapt to the window, unsure of what to expect. Not seeing anything, he walked outside to the lawn. He stood on the grass, enjoying the feel of the cool blades poking between his toes. The rain began falling quite heavily as Seth stretched out his long arms as if receiving a heavenly blessing.

Mya watched through the window as her peculiar friend was getting soaked. At first she giggled at his childishness, but then began to pity him, realizing he had never experienced rain before. Living underground, there were probably many things he had never had a chance to experience. The rain now seemed like a blessing to her as well.

Seth had hardly noticed that Mya had walked up next him. She didn't say anything, but after a minute, he turned and looked at her. Even though her usually full red hair was now long, wet ringlets, and rainwater was dripping from her chin, he still marveled at her beauty. Seth also could not help but notice how her wet, muslin sun dress clung to her ample breasts and long legs. Mya grabbed him and hugged him saying,

"It's wonderful isn't it? I love the rain!"

"There is so much I want to see." He exclaimed. "Is it possible to see the ocean on our journey to Sinjin's?"

Mya had nearly forgotten about the mysterious man that started this whole search. She desperately wanted to meet up with Sinjin, but also felt compelled, almost obligated to help Seth explore the surface world that he had never seen, and may not ever get another chance to.

"We should leave in the morning. I'll go back to my room and tell Allison she can go back home. Then you and I will set out to find Sinjin."

Chapter 10

"Mya, I've known you for a very long time, and I rarely doubt your gut feelings. But are you sure you know what you are doing?"

"You've seen what this guy can do. I think he's legit. I'll be fine, especially now that I figured out how I can use my cell phone without interference. I'll call you regularly."

Allison was still a little skeptical. But Seth did seem to know a lot about what Mya was experiencing.

"Where are you guys headed to find Sinjin?"

"To a small logging village called Mt. Shasta, in Northern California."

Answered Mya.

It was an emotional departure for both girls, seeing Allison drive away knowing how nervous she was about leaving her behind. But Mya was still very confident in her decision; she had to go on.

Seth and Mya rented a convertible to make their trek; Seth was fascinated by the automatic top, but then he marveled at everything it seemed.

The simplest things, things Mya never gave thought to, intrigued him immensely. Yet he knew so much more than her when it came to nature and her mysteries. Possibly things about her that no one has been able to explain yet.

For the most part, the drive north had been uneventful; time seemed to pass quickly while she learned more about the underground villages and their people.

They had nearly all of the same animals there, chickens, deer, birds, and even buffalo. They farmed with irrigation and artificial light. Light, she was told, was created by huge bells carved somehow from a specific type of crystal. When struck, they emanated white light that simulated the sun's. They did not reproduce any sound though.

Apparently, bells were used for many things, depending on the material they were carved from, and the size. Highly tuned sound and light frequencies were used to create various lights, long distant communicating, healing, protection from invaders, even some forms of travel. While most of it seemed too much like an old science fiction movie, with a little imagination, some of it made practical sense. Especially the way Seth described it. Mya's mind was vividly imagining how it must look there, when without warning the car stalled.

"Out of gas?" Mya exclaimed in surprise.

"I can't be…I had a full tank just an hour ago."

The car slowed as she coasted toward the wide shoulder of the country road. Mya looked over her shoulder, trying to see if there was a gas station nearby. As she started explaining what was wrong, she noticed Seth had an unusually nervous look about him.

"Something is wrong Mya"

"That's what I was telling you, we ran out of gas"

"No…I don't think that is it." He said.

As the car stopped, Mya noticed all of the gauges were dead, there was no electricity to the panel, or even the radio for that matter. She tried turning the ignition; not even a click was heard. Totally dead.

"Let me call triple A and get a tow truck." Suggested Mya.

Pulling the cell phone out of her backpack, she noticed it was dead also. Seth's head was panning all around as if he was looking for something.

"Someone is trying to stop us from reaching Sinjin." Seth explained.

"What? Why? Who is?" Mya blurted.

"I don't know, but I can tell, I can feel them nearby. How close are we to Sinjin's town?" He asked.

"Only about 10 miles" Mya estimated.

"We must find another way to get there. Follow me." Ordered Seth.

Seth scrambled out of the car and ran to the woods; Mya quickly grabbed her backpack and hurried to catch up. His long legs were definitely an advantage, he moved like a stealthy shark in the water, graceful and effortless.

Mya noticed Seth had stopped for a second to look back at her, when a very low vibration enveloped her and took her breath away. Her vision suddenly went blurry and she couldn't move.

The super low hum filled her ears, muffling out any other sounds. Her limbs were immobile, though she strained with every muscle to move, she could not. All of her senses were gone, except her sense of smell. Amongst all of the things affecting her body, she could smell a very strong and distinct odor. It was an unpleasant aroma that reminded her of burnt molasses.

Suddenly, a hand with a very strong grip grabbed her forearm, the vibration and noise had disappeared, and her vision returned. The peculiar odor was replaced again with the familiar smell of pine trees.

It was Seth that had grabbed her.

"They have found you, hold my hand and follow me."

Seth quickly guided her into a small cave he had spotted, never once letting go of her hand. Moving quickly, and still glancing around, he took a bottle from his knapsack. Pouring something into his palms he said.

"This will help protect you and make it harder for them to sense you."

Mya had not said a word since he had freed her. Grabbing her shirt, he accidentally broke a button, as he put his large hand down her shirt, covering her neck and her bare breasts with the oil from the bottle. She was completely startled by his actions, but didn't stop him; she didn't feel like it was an attack of any kind. Seth poured more into his hand and applied it from under her shirt to her solar plexus, down her flat stomach, past the waistband of her sweat shorts to her crotch. Just as quickly as he did that, he made some type of symbol on her forehead and then on the nape of her neck.

The oil had an oddly familiar fragrance to it, and tingled warmly where it had been applied.

Her heart was still pounding and her breathing was rapid, from the short run away from whatever was chasing them; she thought she may hyperventilate.

Seth held her hands and looked deeply into her eyes. He was not saying anything, but somehow began to regulate her pounding chest, slowing her breathing back to normal.

"Mya, you must to stay very close to me, trust me and focus your energy on whatever I ask you to. I will not lose you."

"What is going on? Why would someone want keep us

from Sinjin?"

"I was warned that they may try this. There are some other tribes similar to ours, that are very worried about letting anyone from the surface discover our villages and people. They fear that they will invade us and destroy our way of life. The same way the Native Americans were slaughtered and scattered." He explained.

Since it was getting late, Seth thought they should stay in the cave for the night.

As Mya tried to find a comfortable way to sleep, she watched Seth as he meditated, it seemed as though he was talking with someone...but he was alone. He finally came over to her and lay next to her, she scooted over next to him and held onto his arm. For the first time, she realized how strong and big he was, yet so gentle when he touched her, she felt safer than ever before.

Morning came quickly, and Mya was awakened by Seth's voice.

"We must go now, we must get to Sinjin's"

Mya groaned, "Can't a girl get a bagel and coffee first?"

Chapter 11

C autiously navigating the forest, Mya stayed very close to her protector. For several hours now, they had noticed that someone, or something was following close by. Occasionally they would feel a fast rush of cold air race past them, or cross in front of them. Always accompanied by a trace of the unique odor from before; but it did not deter them from pressing on. Mya was in excellent physical shape, but was tiring; she could not keep his pace.

"I have to stop and catch my breath." She said.

"We can't stop. Here, take some water, we are almost there." He responded.

Her body was saying stop, but her mind knew she could not quit; so she pressed on.

"Look." Seth exclaimed.

"We are there, see that dwelling over there?"

Mya saw the small cabin puffing smoke from the chimney; the lights were just visible as dusk was upon them. Only about a hundred yards to a warm fire and hopefully something to eat. They began to walk much faster when suddenly she stumbled on a stone and fell to the ground. She lost her grip on Seth's hand and was immediately surrounded by the same low vibration that paralyzed her before. Seth turned back to grab her, but this time, something was keeping him from reaching her. She could see the despair in his eyes before her vision faded again. He was so close to getting her to Sinjin, now he may fail.

Mya could not get up, but could barely hear Seth's voice mixed in with the humming in her ears. Seth was now kneeling about ten feet from her, talking with someone, but again, the hum surrounding her kept her from understanding what was being said. Finally, a soft blue light enveloped her and she passed out.

Mya awoke to the smell of fresh baked bread, she was in a dimly lit room, and felt a little confused when she realized that she still could not move her legs, it was if there was a heavy weight on them. Glancing at her feet, she was startled to see a big yellow dog laying on them; that's why she couldn't move.

"Rolex, get down now, let her get up."

It was a woman scolding the dog.

"Where is Seth?" Mya asked in a worried tone.

"I am here"

Mya turned to see her protector sitting behind her.

"I told you, I would not lose you"

The woman added, "He has not left you side once."

"Mya, this is Shastina, she is Sinjin's companion."

Shastina nodded as she handed her a bowl of hot soup.

After taking a few bites, Mya looked around and asked.

"So when do I get to meet the man who dragged me into this craziness?"

From behind her, she heard the voice that she had only

briefly heard on her answering machine.

"Welcome to my home Mya, I am Sinjin."

In the doorway stood a very tall, slender old man, his silvery hair was long and pulled into a ponytail, except some bangs that covered his distinct forehead. His beard was braided in long strands. As she gazed at him, she saw past the deep creases of life on his face, and the wisdom of his cool blue eyes, and saw something.

Spinning back around she shouted.

"Where is my backpack?"

Frantically searching the floor, Seth handed it to her. Mya began pouring the contents out until she came to a book, she opened it and pulled out some old photographs and held one up.

"Is this you?"

Pointing to the tall man standing next to her father.

"Yes." He gently said. "That was very long ago."

Her voice trembling and her hands shaking, she demanded.

"How do you know my father?"

Pausing for a moment, as if reflecting on a fond memory, the mysterious man that had turned her world upside down replied…

"I know him, because…he is my son. I am your grandfather Mya."

Mya couldn't speak; tears welled up in her eyes so rapidly they streamed down her cheeks like rivers of rain.

Mya sat in the large tub; her mind still a bit numb from the news Sinjin gave her. The warm water was relaxing as it cascaded over her shoulders from the ladle in Shastina's hand. It had been sometime since another woman had bathed her, but it seemed like nothing to Shastina, who looked at it more like a ritual. They chatted for a while, Mya asking a few quiet questions, while Shastina tried to reassure her everything was fine. She learned that Shastina had been Sinjin's companion and assistant for nearly twenty years, and that she was from a small tribe of Indians that he had lived with for a few years. Mya could see and feel the deep respect and admiration Shastina had for him. When the bath was over, Shastina had her lay down on a table, and began pouring warm oil over her body, massaging it into her tan skin, it was the same peculiar oil that Seth had rubbed on her in the forest. This time she had time to study the properties of the oil. It was very fine, a thin weight, not like cooking oil, and had a fragrance similar to gardenias, though not as strong. Her skin absorbed it very quickly. When Seth had applied it, he only covered a few places on her body, she would later realize the areas he oiled coincided with the Chakra points on her, Shastina, on the other hand was not missing an inch of her body. Once finished, she was given a long, cotton robe to wear, and then went to join Seth and Sinjin by the fireplace.

"I was not aware that you were the grand daughter of Sinjin, I hope I was not irreverent in any way."

Seth had risen and lowered his head, embarrassed that he was not aware of her lineage.

"Don't be silly." She remarked.

Sinjin invited her to join them.

"Come sit with us Mya, let us talk."

It's about time, she thought, as the elderly man motioned her to the chair next to him.

"I have waited a long time to see you my child, and my soul sings and is relieved at last."

"Why did you wait for so long to call me, and why didn't you tell me who you were in your message?"

"You were too young to understand, and not ready to accept your ancestry."

Replied Sinjin.

"So, let me get this straight. Seth had to come and get me, just so I would meet my Grandfather?"

"No, there is more to our meeting than just that. First of all, because I wanted to meet my son's child. You are the only link to my descendents, just as I am the only link to your ancestors. Secondly, since your father has passed to another life, no one would have been able to teach you about yourself and where you come from. Lastly, your people, our people, need your help."

Mya was still dwelling on the comment Sinjin made, about being the only link between them. She remembered as a small child how her father always said that the family bond is one of the few things nobody can take from you. She thought her family was all gone, now she learned that indeed someone was left. Suddenly the last thing he said sunk in.

"Help you? How can I help you? I'm an interior designer, your people need a new look for your Temples?"

In a quite serious tone, Sinjin explained.

"Your father was the keeper of some very valuable information. His task on the surface was to find and document sacred and special locations on the surface.

We had documents and keys to all of the locations, except the ones that your father had discovered. Someone has stolen them from our Temple; we must find the sites and secure them. Your father was bringing his documents to me when he passed on."

"Wait a minute" Mya shot out of her chair.

Digging through her backpack again, she pulled out the maps she had shown Seth earlier.

"Here, look at these." Laying them at Sinjin's sandal clad feet. "I think he had these with him when they found his body."

Seth quickly turned away so he would not look at the sacred papers he had seen earlier. But Sinjin told him it was alright; he had his blessing to gaze at them with him.

"What do these markings represent?" Mya asked.

"The places where your father marked a 'V', are sacred places on the surface, that are high energy vortexes, where the earth talks to the cosmos. The locations marked by the symbol of a key, are portals. Those marked with an 'O', are tunnel openings."

Mya recognized some of the locations, one was very near where they were now, but several were over the oceans. Many of the places had several of the symbols together.

"What do these symbols mean?" pointing at two that he had not mentioned.

"One of them is where some villages are located, but I do not know the last one."

The last one looked kind of like a spiral inside a triangle, with a stick, or flag coming from one side.

Seth sat quietly, even though he thought he had seen it before, he did not want to interrupt.

After studying the maps, as if trying to memorize it, he folded them up and handed them back to Mya.

"These must be taken back to the Temple of the Ancients, and shown to the council of Priests. Seth, you must take her and the maps."

Seth looked even more surprised than Mya did.

"But the elders will not allow it, she is from the surface" Seth exclaimed in a load whisper. He did not want to be blamed for bringing her there.

"Mya is my granddaughter, no one will argue her heritage or right."

"Hey! Why can't Seth just take it himself?" Mya was

beginning to get nervous.

"It is written in your father's hand, they are a part of you. You must finish his task and return them for him. Besides, it is time you met your people, and they met Sinjin's legacy."

"I understand, I will take her to the village"

Seth bowed to show respect and compliance with the elder's wishes.

It would take two days to prepare for their journey; Sinjin conducted several small ceremonies and prayers for their safe passage and blessings from the ancients. Shastina baked an assortment of breads and packed smoked meats, honey and fruit into their backpacks. They would need to leave very early in the morning, before daybreak, Mya lay awake in her bed, gazing out the window at the night sky, contemplating what she was getting herself into, and how she even ended up here. Her eyes slowly closed as she fell into a deep sleep.

Chapter 12

"It is time. You must go now."

Mya blinked her green eyes open to see all three of them standing over her. As she stood, Sinjin pulled her close and wrapped his long arms around her. She had never known her Grandfather, and now, just as she was meeting him, she was hugging him goodbye. They both hoped it would not be the last one. Seth was anxious to get going, he was beginning to miss his village a little, but was more concerned with the ones that were trying to stop them from getting there.

Mya stayed very close to her guide, remembering what had happened to her the last two times they had found her. Every noise seemed strange and almost threatening, she was really feeling out of her element now.

The horizon was beginning to brighten; deep rose colored streaks of clouds were visible through the tops of the tall pines. She had not given much thought about this being the last sunrise she may experience for awhile, but Seth did and stopped long enough to take it in himself. He took out some bread and honey for their breakfast. Just as she was relaxing, a loud, deep howl let out. It was not a wolf or coyote type, much deeper and somehow sad sounding. Mya looked at Seth for reassurance.

"We are getting close, those are warnings from the guardians"

"Guardians? Who are they?"

"When anyone gets close to the openings, they alert us and then distract the intruders so they can not find a way in"

"Are they men or animals? It sounds like an animal"

With a small smile Seth said, "I don't know. I've never seen one."

They continued through the thick brush and dense trees. Mya couldn't see any path they were on, but Seth definitely knew where he has headed. The air became cooler and she could hear the sound of rushing water, like a waterfall. Seth let her know they were close; Mya's heart began quickening in anticipation. A large cloud of mist appeared from behind a few large ferns. As they got closer, the mist began clinging to their clothes and hair; it was very refreshing from the long hike. Holding Seth's hand tightly, she felt him pull her behind the falls.

The water was not cascading into a river, but went straight down into a dark, moss covered hole, and Mya strained to see the bottom, but could not. They were standing behind the falls in a narrow cave; it was quite dark, though some type of light source was coming from far away. As her eyes adjusted, she could see faint carvings and paintings on the cave's walls, similar to Petroglyphs she had seen in National Geographic magazines. Seth was walking rather swiftly, so she couldn't focus too much on the carvings, or she may stumble. Mya could tell they were descending at a fairly good rate, but had no way to gage how deep under the surface they were. She began studying the cave walls and floor as they progressed, was this a natural or man made cave? She wondered. The sides were relatively smooth, either carved by a powerful tool, or maybe lava tunnels, this was after all a dormant volcano.

"Stop, watch your step here."

Seth pointed to the floor six feet ahead. It disappeared. In front of them, Mya saw the wide crevice that interrupted their path.

Off to one side, she noticed a rope bridge draping across the bottomless gap.

"Is that how we get over there?"

Seth just nodded his head; but something did not seem right. He distinctly remembered lowering the rope when he got to this side. Someone had crossed it since he had been there, and had left it up. He knelt down at the foot of the bridge and stared.

"What is it?" asked Mya.

"Footprints. They are going across to the village, not coming from it. It looks like several sets."

Mya could see the concern come over his face, and that made her nervous.

"I will cross first, then you follow." He said.

Seth tested the bridge with one foot, not wanting to put too much weight on it at first. It felt strong enough, so he cautiously proceeded. Once he reached the other side he waived her over, then began looking at the floor again.

The rope beneath her feet seemed to sway much more than it did with Seth. The rope was wet and a little slippery; her hands were perspiring as well, which made it difficult to hang on to the upper rope. Seth hardly noticed that she was across and standing behind him. He was crouched down looking at footprints. Pointing to his right, he said.

"The footprints all head that direction. The village is this way though." Now pointing his long arm to the left.

Whoever is was, they did not go to the village, Seth did not know where the other path led. Grabbing Mya's hand, they headed to the village. It was not very much further when they came to the end of the tunnel. The walls were covered in vines which Seth parted, revealing a beautiful valley below them. It was like stepping into a botanical garden, lush plants, trees, and fragrant flowers. One of the first things Mya noticed was the soft shadows; no real shade under the trees. There was no sun, just an ambient, soft light emanating from above.

"My village is this way." Seth began following the small dirt pathway down. Rounding a corner, Mya saw the most perfect little lake below them. The water was a piercing blue, and very inviting, but something seemed peculiar. The water wasn't moving, not even a ripple. Then she realized there was no wind to create any waves, that's why it was so calm. She couldn't help but think about how fun it would be to water ski across it.

Seth's expression seemed stoic; she thought he would be getting more excited as the got closer to his home. Maybe he was disappointed because there was no welcoming party. Suddenly they stopped, before them was a sight no one from the surface had ever been allowed to see. There were several simple, but sturdy huts set in a circular pattern, with some larger structures in the distance. Seth had done a good job describing it to her, although it was much larger and more organized the she had expected. The plants were so plentiful and large; Mya truly was in awe. She put her arms around Seth and squeezed him. Looking up at him she beamed.

"It's wonderful Seth."

But her excitement faded quickly when she saw his

eyes staring at his village. She knew something was wrong.

"They are all gone. There is no one here." Declared Seth.

Looking back at the huts, she then noticed that there were no people, no sounds.

Walking through the deserted village, they peered into the homes of his family and friends, wondering what happened. There was no destruction, no signs of violence, no clues at all.

"Let's go look in the Temple." Seth suggested.

As they approached the sacred building, Seth knelt down to pray and pay respect to the Ancients, Mya knelt down behind him, following his lead. Inside the spacious building, Mya was amazed at how many different cultural styles there were. Hieroglyphics, Cretan style paintings, even Mayan type drawings. Some things that made absolutely no sense to her at all, but that was no surprise.

"The Knowledge Crystal is gone..." Seth exclaimed.

"...the villagers would not stay here without it. Whoever took it, took the village with them."

Seth stared at the empty altar that once proudly held the sacred object. The room looked so sterile and cold to him. Walking up beside her stunned friend, Mya asked,

"Obviously it was very important to your village. What is this 'Knowledge Crystal'?"

"It is the most ancient and important part of our history...your history. It is a very sacred crystal, the most beautiful blue color you have seen. All of our history, our emotions, experiences, writings from the ancients are all inside it."

Seth could see that Mya was trying to understand him, but was not grasping it.

"All objects of nature retain imprints of natural energy, in addition to their own. Metals, trees, stones, even water and the air around us can hold information imprinted in it. But crystals can hold vast amounts more and much more detail. Even in your world, nothing is more accurate for storing information and timing than crystal. Your watches and computers have crystals in them."

Mya nodded as she listened intently. Seth pulled a small crystal from his pocket and offered it to her. As she held it, Seth placed his hands around hers.

"Close your eyes, focus your mind on the quartz. Tell me Mya, what do you see?"

Slowly opening her eyes, she lifted her gaze up to him.

"My father..."

"When you touched this, the image in your soul was deposited and recorded into the crystal, it is here forever now." Seth explained.

"And that is what the missing crystal does?"

"The Knowledge Crystal is like a library of immense size and importance. Our ancestors, other's ancestors, secrets of the cosmos and all that reside there, have used it to record their knowledge."

Mya was quickly realizing the impact that this object has had, and will have on all civilizations. She was finally beginning to feel a connection with her ancestry, and it was overwhelming.

As they walked toward the large archway to leave the Temple, Seth stopped as if he had heard something; Mya stopped also to see what he was looking at.

In the shadows off to one of the hallways, they both saw someone step back behind a pillar. Seth slowly walked toward the figure, when it whispered,

"Seth? It is you? I knew you would return!"

"Lemule? Why do you hide? What has happened?"

Lemule remained in the shadows; he did not want to be

seen by the stranger with his old friend.

"Come out here Lemule, greet me."

Slowly, cautiously, he stepped out to greet Seth, who had noticed that Lemule's eyes never left Mya.

"She is from the surface, she should not be here or see us!" Lemule whispered nervously.

"Its okay, come here."

Seth grabbed his hand and led him over to her.

"This is my good friend Lemule, we have been friends since we were small children. Lemule, this is Mya. She is why I was sent on my journey, Mya is Sinjin's granddaughter."

Lemule's eyes widened and looked at Seth in amazement. He lowered his eyes and dropped to his knees in respect.

"Forgive my rudeness, I did not know."

Mya gave a puzzled look at Seth and reached down for Lemule's hands.

"It's okay, please stand, you couldn't know. Hell, I didn't know until a few days ago!"

The three of them sat under a large willow tree on the side of the lake, Lemule telling the others what had happened. How only a few days before, Travelers secretly entered the village and stole the Knowledge Crystal and took some of the elders with them. They tried to follow them, but they seemed to just fade into the mountainsides, and since their maps had been stolen earlier, they did not know how to follow them.

"What happened to Kira? Did they take her too?" Seth asked.

"No, the Priestess escaped and took the rest of the villagers and the children to other villages."

As they sat and pondered what to do, Mya stood up and announced she was going to take a dip in the lake. She was not used to the humidity of the underground air, and the cool water was very inviting. Sliding out of her long cotton dress, she looked over her shoulder.

"Anyone care to join me?"

The guys stared at her naked body as she prepared to dive in. She stood on a small rock at the water's edge but hesitated to jump in.

"Are there fish in there?" Mya was concentrating, trying to see into the lake.

"Not in those waters" Seth remarked.

Mya began backing away from the shore. There were very small ripples appearing on the surface of the water, and they were growing in size. If there were no fish, and no wind to move the water...

"Something is down there...and I think it's coming up!"

Seth jumped up, grabbed her hand and pulled her away from the edge. Scooping up her dress and backpack, they all scrambled away from the lake.

Lemule quickly led them to a nearby waterfall where they hid between the cascading water and the rock wall behind it. The constant roar of the fall was not loud enough to drown out the sound of her own pounding heart, as Mya tried to put her wet dress on without giving away their hiding place.

The once, mirror like lake was now bubbling wildly as something was emerging from the water. It was difficult to see through the ribbons of water racing in front of their faces, but they could see enough to make out a tall figure walking out of the lake right where they had been sitting.

"It is one of the Travelers" Lemule could barely get the words out.

The Traveler took a few steps, stopped and looked in all

directions of the valley, then proceeded right toward their waterfall. Mya was more nervous than she had ever been, she squeezed Seth's large hand so tight she thought she make break it.

"Concentrate, match my energy level."

Mya slowly reached up and clutched her father's pendant that hung around her heaving chest.

As the Traveler got closer to them, she seemed to calm down, her heart, that had felt like it was going to leap from her body was now beating at a soft easy rhythm. It felt as though they had melted into the wet wall behind them. Mya was now amazingly calm as the strange figure walked right up to the waterfall. She strained to see through the wall of water that separated them by less than three feet.

The Traveler was very tall, probably seven feet in height, very broad shoulders, though not too muscular, more lean. It's arms and legs were quite long, she could not make out its hands through the water. What struck her as even more peculiar, was the lack of facial features, the shape of its head, rather narrow and sleek, and it's skin, the color of moss yet shimmery. The Traveler made no sound, but she suddenly felt a strong pulse that shot through the liquid barrier and passed right through them. With the sensation of the surge of energy that just passed through her, something else grabbed Mya's attention. The smell of burnt molasses. The Traveler stared right into the waterfall and then turned away, walking back up to the Temple.

"It didn't see us!" Mya whispered with surprise.

They peeked out from their hiding place to see what it was up to. The gangly being had entered the Temple as if he knew where he was going. Before the trio made it back out into the clear, the intruder re-emerged from the sacred building, as if he had been interrupted. Quickly they jumped back into hiding as the Traveler hurriedly headed back towards the lake. He moved very gracefully, but covered a large area without looking like a run. Without hesitation, walked right into the lake and disappeared. The pristine waters were once again, perfectly still.

"It was obviously looking for something, maybe they left something behind?" Mya proposed.

"But why did it leave so abruptly?"

"Maybe it was called back? It didn't spend much time looking around."

Curious to find out why the Traveler came back, the three of them headed back to the Temple. Inside they inspected every hall and column for clues, but found nothing that may have been dropped or left behind. Just as they were about to head out. Lemule shouted.

"Over here, I don't remember this doorway being open before, do you?"

Seth agreed as they looked at the enormous door made of stone. It was more like a wall on a hinge, a secret passage way perhaps, but leading where? A soft light could be seen from the slight opening, neither of them knew of that room, though Seth had spent great amounts of time in the Temple studying with the Teachers.

"Well, there is only one way to find out…right? Mya asked as she tried prying the heavy door open.

"It is probably a sacred place, only the Elders should go in there" Lemule exclaimed.

"I believe that the Elders are in need of our help" answered Seth, "and if there is something in there that can help us…we must go"

Saying prayers and asking forgiveness from the Ancients, Lemule followed his partners.

The passageway continued downward in a slow, lazy spiral. The granite steps and walls were gently illuminated by bluish crystal imbedded in the walls. Nearing the end of the passage, bronze and gold plates with inscriptions began appearing on the walls. Lemule began chanting and praying faster, for he knew by the inscriptions, that the Ancients wrote them.

"I have never seen this type of language." Mya remarked. "Seth, do you know what it is?"

"These are Akashic writings…very, very old. Only the most wise and venerable know how to read them."

The end of the passageway opened to a large vault; the walls were encased in gold, which had more engravings on it. It was the dome shaped ceiling that really got Mya's attention. Paintings of amazing detail and brilliance covered the entire span; it reminded her of the great Italian churches. Even Seth and Lemule were in awe; this was their history. The paintings described their ancestor's journey from their homeland, maps of the skies and stars, and strange labyrinth like symbols. In the center of the room, stood a low altar that was now bare; someone had taken something from it in haste, knocking some ceremonial stones and statuettes to the floor. While trying to make sense of the engravings on the walls, Mya noticed a green, baseball size crystal, protruding slightly from the top of the wall where it met the ceiling. She realized that it was actually sitting atop a recessed pole that blended into the wall itself. Following a line directly across the room, was another, then she found another pair, and another, a total of six. Upon closer examination, Seth realized that the poles were hinged at the bottom. With the help of Lemule, they lowered one at a time until all six pointed at each other in the center of the room. Once they were all in position, each crystal began to glow and radiate light in the direction of the crystal opposite it. The pale blue lights slowly stretched across the opening, until they met each other like thin, outstretched fingers. All looked with amazement and wondered what it's function was, when

Lemule walked to the center of the six spoked star of light, and instantly disappeared.

"Lemule!" They both yelled simultaneously.

"Where did he go Seth? What is this thing?"

"It must be a portal, and I have no idea where it leads to."

"How do we get him back? Should we follow him?"

"No, we should focus our energy on the finding the Elders and villagers first. We will leave the portal open so Lemule can get home."

Crawling under the poles, they made their way to the staircase, avoiding the chance of being caught in the rays of the portal. Following Seth up the stairs of the gilded passage, Mya looked over her shoulder at the portal, she worried if Lemule would find his way back, or would someone else emerge uninvited.

Once they reached the Altar room of the Temple, Seth said he would need to meditate to try and find the others. He went to the center of the room, knelt down, and began softly reciting a mantra in a language she could not understand. Mya stayed back from Seth, so as not to disturb him. While he remained in his trance, Mya wandered the Temple rooms, trying to understand the inscriptions and engravings that adorned the walls and ceilings. She had never seen anything so elegant and detailed,; every inch was a masterpiece. The silence was interrupted when Seth shouted.

"I know where they are!"

Mya spun around and headed back into the main chamber.

"A neighboring village has taken them in. All of the children, some of the villagers and Kira; she is safe. We must go to them, quickly."

They grabbed their knapsacks and filled them with fruits and vegetables from the village storerooms before heading out.

Mya was surprised that another settlement existed under the surface, but soon learned that in fact there were many civilizations that existed underground, undetected by the 'modern world'.

Chapter 13

As they walked towards what seemed like a vine covered dead end; Seth led Mya behind a curtain of tangled spanish moss and ivy, revealing the mouth of a cave. The same, soft, hazy light she saw in the other passageway dimly illuminated the tunnel. This tunnel was quite different though. Unlike the carved and adorned walls before, these had a natural rolling surface, not chiseled, but glossy like glass.

"Are these lava tubes?" Mya asked.

"Yes, there are thousand of them that lace many of the villages together. Many are unknown by most, so they use the passageways made by the ancients."

"How can you tell where you are going? There are no signs; do you have a map?"

"Only a few maps have been drawn, your father had done some of them. The best way to know where you are going, is to know where others have been. Let your body hear the footsteps of the ancients and of those who have stepped where your feet are now."

It all sounded a bit cheesy, and she felt like teasing him, but considering the fact that she had no idea where she was, she best keep her sarcasm to herself and learn.

After hiking for what seemed about 45 minutes, the pair came to an intersection of sorts, where there were now three choices of tunnels, one of which looked as though it had been carved, like the first one, it joined into the chamber they were in from above.

"Well, this is interesting, which one do we take?" Mya asked while surveying the options.

"This one is a passageway to the surface, we don't want that one." Seth exclaimed, pointing to the one that someone had carved.

As they both concentrated on the choices, Mya began walking to the opening on the right.

"This one, I believe this is it."

Seth was going to question her, but he knew that the female's intuition was stronger than a man's, and knowing the abilities of her family line, he would accept her choice without hesitation.

Soon they were feeling a gentle breeze blowing in their faces, and an increase in humidity, a sure sign they were nearing an opening to a settlement. Tightly grasping his hand, Mya followed Seth into the cavernous opening. She was surprised to see different types of dwellings than the other village, there was not as many and did not see any Temple type buildings. With Seth in front, they slowly walked to the center of what looked like a town plaza, and stopped. No villagers could be seen, Mya thought the worst; that the Travelers had gotten there first. But then, a tall, slender woman dressed in a long smooth white dress, emerged from one of the buildings, and slowly walked toward them.

The woman walked with such grace and confidence, anyone could tell she held some position of importance. Her hair was long, red and flowing, very much like her own, except it had thin, gold ribbons woven throughout, and a simple gold and jeweled crown resting atop. Seth slowly dropped to his knees as she approached, instinctively, Mya did the same.

"Seth, I am so pleased to see you here, safe. Please rise and introduce me to our guest."

"Kira, this is Mya, I was instructed to bring her to our village to continue her father's work and teach her our heritage. She is Sinjin's granddaughter, she is Lemurian."

Kira stretched out her hands and held Mya's to welcome her. Kira, the Lemurian Priestess, then bent a knee, lowered her eyes, and spoke warmingly.

"Mya, I am honored."

"The honor is indeed mine." Mya replied, though thinking to herself, why would she be honored to meet me?

Mya still did not understand the importance of who she was, and who her grandfather was. As she lifted her eyes, she could see the other villagers had emerged from their hiding places, and about 12 young children were running to embrace a village friend and legend, Seth. Their small, but enthusiastic smiles and giggles were so refreshing to Mya. As they laughed and played, several of them looked at Mya with curiosity. They knew she was not a villager, and that outsiders were strictly forbidden.

Kira took them into a large dwelling; a gathering room of sorts, where she had some girls bring fruit, hot bread and tea to drink. Kira told them of the invasion and their fortunate escape, and discussed what needed to be done. She also asked about Lemule, she knew he had stayed and waited for Seth. When they told her about the secret chamber and portal that Lemule disappeared from, Kira's eyes lowered, then asked if they had closed the portal before leaving. Apparently, they should have. But there were other priorities, the first was to find and return the Crystal of Knowledge, then, locate all of the vortexes, passageways and portals.

"Mya." Kira explained. "Your father was working on a very important mission while on the surface. He, like your grandfather, and like yourself, have an extremely high sensitivity to energy fields and specific patterns, or cosmic shadows, if you will. When Sinjin became too old, your father continued the work."

"What work was that? My father liked geology."

She had already been given an explanation from Sinjin, but wanted to see if Kira had a different story.

"He was locating and mapping all of the known, and discovering unknown portals and vortexes. There are others who are wishing to use them to destroy our civilizations, by giving the locations to the scientists of the surface people. They will certainly seek us out and expose us. Our existence, culture and knowledge will all but disappear."

"But how will you keep the others from exposing the entrances, just by us knowing where they are?"

"We can hide, and de-activate them, from the Temple of The Ancients, with a stone key that your father had; it is the only one."

Mya instantly thought of the contents in her knapsack, the maps she couldn't read, and the collection of stones.

"There is one other thing about your father's quest I must tell you. Many years ago, a thief took a most sacred article from the Temple, the FireStone. It is the most powerful stone known. There is a small hidden deposit deep in the earth; the location is inscribed on the FireStone itself, written in a most ancient script to keep it from being found. It is rumored that your father found the FireStone on his journey and hid it at one of the places on the map until he could retrieve it. We also believe that he hid the stone key there. We can not close all of the portals without it. He, and now you Mya, are the only ones that have the power to locate it's energy vibration."

Mya looked over at Seth, even he looked amazed, he had no idea Mya had such powers either. He was finally realizing why the Elders placed such importance and responsibility on him for finding her.

Feeling Mya's nervousness, Kira had some of the girls bring in a special hot tea for them all.

"Let us all relax now, and celebrate our new found sister."

One of the girls handed a large cup carved from a gourd to Mya, and then the others. Pursing her lips and blowing the steam from the heady brew, she drew in a sip. The taste was slightly pungent, yet a little familiar.

"May I ask what this made from?" Asked Mya.

"It is Kava, a root, sweetened with honey. Do you like it?" Kira asked.

Mya laughed. "Kava? I drink this at home all the time to relax."

Maybe their differences were not so great after all.

Some of the children had joined them and played flutes and danced with each other around the fire. When they finished the music, the children left and some young women came in carrying vases, filled with oil. A few went to Kira's side and Seth's side, and the others came to her. As they knelt next to her, they begin removing her robe; she looked over to see Kira and Seth were getting the same treatment.

Mya had always enjoyed a good massage, but had never been massaged by three pairs of women's hands. It was a scene she would never had thought herself in, except in one of her fantasies. She felt oddly comfortable, not the least bit embarrassed, lying totally nude in a room with other nude people, with six hands covering her body with warm oil. Maybe it was the Kava tea, which was a hundred times more potent than was she was used to, or the atmosphere that made her massage seem much more erotic than she had expected. The look in a few of her topless attendant's eyes, as they brushed against her, seemed to confirm her feelings.

Mya woke to the voice of a child offering her some fruit. She was in the same room, alone, but still unclothed; she reached for her robe to cover up in front of the child, who thought it was strange to try to hide her body. A naked body is not a novelty or taboo to every culture; how refreshing she thought.

Walking across the plaza to the well, everyone seemed so joyous, especially the children, maybe they were not aware of their situation. Splashing water on her face, she recognized one of the young women that massaged her last night, was doing the same.

"Good morning Mya. Did you sleep well last night?"

"Very well, thank you."

The beautiful young woman smiled demurely and walked away. What did I do last night? She thought.

Kira studied the drawings and maps that Mya pulled from her knapsack, while Seth asked questions.

"Kira, there are no Elders here, what happened to them?"

"Some were taken by the Travelers, others may have gone off on their own. But all are unhurt. I can tell."

"There is much work for us to do, what shall we do first Priestess?" Seth asked.

"The both of you must locate the Knowledge Crystal first, and return it to the Temple. Seth you must now also become Teacher for Mya. Help her to harness the powers she owns and to become a strong part of Nature's mysticism. Then use the drawings to help you find the FireStone and bring it back safely. Use the portals as you need to, and close the ones you don't. Remember, your ancestors, the Ancients, and all of the cosmos are at your call; use them."

Packing up her maps and stones, Mya was eager to get going. Their first destination was a portal that seemed thousands of miles away on the map.

"It will take us forever to walk that distance." Mya announced.

"You will find a way, you will need to use that portal to get to wherever they have hidden the Crystal." Instructed Kira.

Chapter 14

Walking through an endless labyrinth of tunnels, Mya often thought to herself, if Seth actually knew where he was headed, but considering all of the amazing things she had witnessed, she knew she had better trust his instincts.

"Seth…what is that noise I keep hearing?"

Seth stopped and looked around.

"I do not hear anything Mya"

"It's a low rumbling kind of sound, coming from either right above us or ahead of us"

Seth looked puzzled; he couldn't hear what she was hearing.

"Don't you feel it under your feet?" Placing her hands against the cold stone walls, and then sliding them toward the tunnel ceiling, she could feel the low reverberations clearly. Seth began feeling the walls also, but only experienced the coldness of the stone.

"This must be the sensitivity Kira spoke of", Seth reminded her.

"Only you and your father would have been able to sense this frequency"

It was so strong a feeling, she couldn't believe Seth could not sense it.

"You take the lead now Mya, follow your senses to the source."

Mya followed the rumble past a few other junctures, when suddenly they walked into a large room with a few tunnels joining from the other side and two more at the top of the room. In the center of the room was a small vehicle of some kind.

They both approached it cautiously, looking around the room for its driver.

It reminded Mya of a roller coaster car from an amusement park, about the same size, but no wheels or rails to ride on. There was no steering wheel to speak of, no seats, and only a cavity big enough for a couple of people. It was not carved of wood; it looked more like a plastic. Looking at each other, they both climbed inside.

There were no instruments, no levers, no pedals, and just a simple box like tray in the center.

"Maybe my father's notes will give us a clue."

Emptying her knapsack on the floor of the dormant sled, Mya rummaged through all of the papers she had brought. Suddenly, the little craft jumped up off of the ground, and the tray lit up, but then settled back down and went dormant again.

"You must have hit a switch or something when you emptied your bag."

Leaning over to clear the floor and look for a switch, the same thing happened again, the craft rose and then went right back down. It was if someone was playing with a light switch. The next time it went up, Seth commanded, "Don't

move. You have the key, it's hanging around your neck."
Mya looked down, and sure enough, the satchel she had
hung around her neck carrying her father's stone collection,
was dangling right above the tray.

"One of these stones must be activating it."
Opening the drawstring, Mya could see one smooth little stone was glowing the same color as the tray. She placed
it in the tray and the little sled came to life.

They still were not moving, just kind of hovering.
"Okay, now what? How do we make it move and which
way are we going?"

"I think it will take us wherever you want it to. Just focus on our destination. Concentrate as I taught you before."

Mya began to visualize the location on the map, putting
herself in a meditative state. Within seconds, their tiny car
rose higher and headed for one of the upper tunnels, upon
entering it shot off with lightening quickness. Unlike the
lava tubes and tunnels they had been hiking through, this
one was pitch black; they could not see anything. Mya
knew they were moving at a high rate of speed, as her long
hair was whipping around and hitting Seth in the face. She
reached back and nervously searched for his comforting
hand to squeeze. They did not talk much, perhaps out of
anxiousness; they listened to odd noises as they whisked
past occasional lights, indicating a tunnel juncture, the sled
itself made no noise at all.

Forty-five minutes had passed when the sled began
slowing down, then popped up into a softly lit cavern and
stopped. Rubbing their eyes, and squinting to adjust to the
sudden emergence from darkness, they grabbed their belongings and hopped out, Mya reached back inside.

"I better not forget this", she exclaimed, holding up the
stone that activated the sled.

The chamber was much larger than the first, and had

many more tunnels joining it, much like a train hub. There were a few other sleds in the chamber, but no people to be seen. Mya had no idea as to where they were, or how deep into the earth they had traveled. Both had agreed that this must be some sort of traffic intersection, kind of like a bus or train station. Looking at her father's map, Mya began noticing markings that were located on some of the tunnel overheads, they were road signs. She began laying out a plan.

"We know where we started on the map, but don't know where we are right now. We do know how long it took to get here though, so I think we should head for the most distant location, calculate our total travel time, which will give us some idea of how long it will take to get to each portal. If we are lucky, we will find what we came for at the next stop. Look for the tunnel with this symbol above it."

Many of the symbols carved into the stone were faded and difficult to identify, but soon Seth was shouting that he had found it. This particular tunnel entrance was high up in the cave's ceiling, and had a sled below it. As they both crawled inside, Mya pulled out the stone that had activated the first one, put it the holder, and once again, was lifted off the ground. This time however, a glass shield popped up from the sides and enclosed them. As they sped up towards the mouth of the tunnel, they could see something inside, a wall of water, and the sled was speeding right towards it.

Mya reached for Seth's arm and closed her eyes anticipating the impact, only to realize that the sled simply passed right through it without notice. It took a second before she realized where they were.

"We're underwater! Look at all the fish, and seaweed, it must be the ocean, not a lake."

Looking up through the glass dome that sealed the sled,

Mya realized it was fairly light, they must not be too deep, otherwise it would be pitch black. The water was also extremely clear, like you might see in the Bahamas, she had no idea which ocean they were in.

Within a few seconds, the light around them began diminishing; they were now diving deeper. Both of them were beginning to get a little disoriented in the inky blackness that surrounded them, when a streak of light crossed in front of them, the another. As they continued to the bottom of the sea, small clusters of lights began appearing, with more streaks of light going in and out of them.

"It's a city, or a colony of some sort." Mya exclaimed.

"Water dwellers. I have heard stories of them" Seth had never thought he would see them, let alone be headed right for their city.

Chapter 15

Allison let herself into Mya's apartment to drop off the mail that had been collecting in her box, only to find that it had been ransacked. Everything seemed to have been overturned or opened, as if someone had been franticly searching for something. At first she was angry, but anger soon turned to concern and fear for her friend. Was it Seth? Had he been here before they had met? Or even worse, after? He seemed pretty harmless though; it couldn't have been him. Who ever it was, seemed to have an interest in books though. As she looked around, most of the mess was centered around her desk and bookshelves. It wasn't a robbery, her TV, stereo and artwork were still there; someone was obviously hunting for something in particular. Aside from the disheveled mess caused by someone's search, only one other thing seemed unusual…a lingering smell of burnt molasses.

She assumed it was coming from the neighboring apartment, after checking the kitchen. Allison left, locking the door behind her, unsure as to whether she should call the police or not. All the way back to her own apartment, she tried to reach her friend on her cell phone, only to keep getting her voice mail.

"Mya, this is Allison. It's really important that you call me as soon as you get this message, please call me and let me know where you are and that you are okay."

Sitting in front of her fireplace, Allison sipped a glass of Merlot, and tried to imagine where Mya might be and why anyone would rummage through her desk. What was they were looking for? As she readied for bed, she noticed something reflecting from the floor as she turned back the covers. It looked like a card size brass template, with an intricately carved out symbol in the middle of it. Allison recognized it as a bookmark that had been in one of Mya's father's books she had laid on her bed.

Was this what they were looking for? Did Mya need this with her? If it were important enough for someone to break into her apartment, then what would they do to Mya if they found her? What would they do if they knew she had it here? Allison knew she couldn't wait for Mya to return, she had to go and find her and give her the brass template. There was only one person that could tell her where Mya was…Sinjin.

She remembered that her friend had told her that she and Seth were going to meet him in northern California, a town called Mt. Shasta, so that's where she would go.

Chapter 16

The trip took her two days, through the high deserts of Utah, and over the Sierra Nevada mountain range, and into the fertile Napa Valley. A winery tour seemed perfect, but she knew she there was no time to stop. As she pulled off of the interstate, to the entrance of the old town, she couldn't imagine why anyone from this part of the state would want Mya. The sleepy little logging community seemed to have been settled right at the foot of the huge extinct volcano that gave the town it's name, as if to honor it or guard it.

Allison stopped in a small coffee shop to get a flavor for the town. There she began to notice the eclectic collection of calendars, postcards and books on the region. Books that told of strange legends and cults that gravitated to the mountain, how the mountain itself created it's own weather patterns. For such odd souvenirs reflecting the town, the people seemed very friendly and down to earth. Knowing it was a longshot, Allison asked the clerk if she knew a man in town by the name of Sinjin, the young man politely said he did not, but maybe she could ask someone that had lived here longer. He suggested the city park, lots of old people hang out there.

At the park, there were a few kids riding and trying to jump their skateboards, lovers giggling on blankets spread on the lawn, and some joggers, but no old men playing checkers or anything like that. It looked like a typical small town America city park. Wandering in the vast cool shade being cast under huge, ancient trees, Allison spied an old bag lady, having a good time sharing some crumbs with a squirrel. At first, she was going to pass her by, but then remembered something she had heard on a TV show about the homeless. 'The unseen, see more than the ones that ignore them'.

I'll bet she knows everything about this town, she thought to herself.

The old woman's eyes were wide, and sparkling, her face seemed to have wrinkles on top of wrinkles, probably from years of living in the open. Her fingers were long and slender, but bent unmercifully by arthritis. She looked like she could have been a dancer or pianist many years ago. Allison felt empathy for her, wondering if she was a grandmother and if her family knew how she was living.

"Excuse me ma'am, I was wondering if you could tell me where I might find a man that lives in this town. His name is Sinjin"

For a moment, the woman stopped feeding her little friend, and then looked up at Allison.

"Have you come for him? To try to take him away?"

"I don't want to take him anywhere. I just want to talk to him about a friend of mine that came to visit him"

"Well, Sinjin does not have many visitors, nor does he

see many. Too many questions, they ask…all those nosey tourists."

A peculiar statement, Allison thought.

"Sinjin lives in the woods, off of the Twin Mines road. Maybe if he saw your friend, he will see you too."

"Thank you kindly ma'am."

Allison reached into her pocket and handed her a ten-dollar bill for her help.

"Oh missy, I don't need any money…but maybe I can buy some bread for my friends here. Thank you"

Twin Mines road was about six miles north of the town. It was nothing more than a dirt road with no markings used to access some old defunct mines. After several bumpy minutes, a small cabin could be seen at the end of an even more secluded dirt road. There were no address markers or mailboxes to indicate whom lived there, but figured it must be the place, there were no other houses in the area.

As she got closer to the cabin, a woman stepped out onto the porch and then walked over to her.

"Can I help you?" the woman asked.

"I'm looking for a man named Sinjin, I was told I could find him here"

"I am sorry, he is very busy and does not want to be disturbed. Thank you"

The robed lady then turned and walked back toward the cabin, indicating to Allison that she should leave.

"Wait! You don't understand. My best friend, Mya, was coming here with a guy named Seth, at Sinjin's request. I must talk with him now!"

Allison did not come this far just to be shot down.

The woman stopped in her tracks and turned around.

"You are a friend of Mya's, and you know Seth?"

"Yes."

Shastina looked around the area, as if checking to see if

anyone else was there.

"Come." She motioned Allison to follow her into the cabin.

Allison waited in the first room, while Shastina spoke to Sinjin in the other room. After a moment, she was waved in to see him.

"You are a friend of Mya's?"

"Yes, my name is Allison, and I need to find her and talk to her right away."

"Mya is with Seth on a journey right now. Why is it so important that you came her to talk with her?"

"Look, I don't know who you are, and what all is going on, only what Seth told us, and that someone is looking for her or something she has."

Sinjin's expression turned to concern.

"Do you think she is in danger?"

"I'm worried for her. Someone broke into her apartment and was looking for something. I think this is what that wanted. It was part of her father's belongings, and she left it at my house"

Allison held up the metal template for him to examine.

"Indeed she will need this, and several people would like to prevent her from getting it. We must find a place to meet her.

Shastina, please take Allison in the other room while I try to contact Mya."

The heavy door gently closed behind them to allow total concentration by Sinjin. He took up his usual position in front of the fire, and quickly slipped into a meditative state. Low chanting could be heard through the heavy wooden door, but she could not tell what he was actually saying.

Allison paced by the window while she waited, staring out at the dense forest, watching the squirrels scurrying about, when she noticed that the beams of sunlight filtering down through the tree tops began to dim. Was it that late in the afternoon? Was the sun setting already? Allison looked at her watch to discover it was only 2:30 in the afternoon, so why was it getting darker? Within a few seconds, she noticed a heavy fog drifting toward the cabin, which seemed odd this time of year, and the fact that it was perfectly clear when she arrived. Once the cabin was completely enveloped in the murky mist, the fog began to change color; a faint greenish blue color began to take over the drab gray surrounding. Looking back at Shastina, Allison asked.

"Does this happen regularly up here?"

She could tell by her expression it did not.

"Should we tell Sinjin?"

"No, we must not interrupt him."

She replied, as she moved next to the door, as if to guard it. Moments later, the swamp colored fog began creeping under the doorway, moving, undulating slowly as if seeking out a prey. A very low hum could be heard as more of the heavy mist began to permeate through the cracks around the windows and door. Allison was shocked and becoming anxious, she had never seen such a thing. She turned her head to see what Shastina was doing, and to strongly suggest they interrupt Sinjin, when she realized she could barely move her head. It felt as if everything had slowed to super slow motion, taking great effort to swivel her head. Shastina's position next to the door seemed frozen, as did her expression. Allison could not move either, just a very slow and limited turn of her head; she could not speak either. She tried desperately to understand what was going on, but her mind had slowed down as much as the rest of her, all she could do is observe the weird things happening around her.

The mist that had seeped into the cabin seemed to break

off into wisps, like smoke, that swirled around the room, hunting for something. They swirled around Allison like a mini tornado, then slowly again, darting between her legs, slithering around her body and around her neck, like a large snake made of smoke. She felt nothing but breezes as it passed around her, strong enough to move her hair.

The little wisps of mist, then did the same to Shastina across the room. She could see her long coal black hair being tossed around like she was standing near a fan, she did not utter a word or move at all either. After exploring the rest of the room, they slowed down their frantic maneuvers and merge into a single, larger drift, and slowly headed for the door that Sinjin was meditating behind. She worried for the old man, he seemed so frail, he might have a heart attack. Soon bright shafts of light began bursting through the cracks of the wooden door, the beams wrapped around Shastina, making her appear like an angel; the hum increased as the entire room was now glowing white. Allison could no longer make out any details in the room; she had been enveloped in the bright fog, leaving her void of any sense of depth, direction, sight, or movement. Her mind continued to fight for the ability to reason, was she dying, was she in a coma, or dreaming? Soon, her concentration faded and she slipped into a comfortable numbness.

Chapter 17

As they neared the underwater complex, Mya asked. "What do you know of the water dwellers?"

"Like you and me, the are descendants of an ancient people. They left their homes on the surface to escape the fire from the sky, and to hide from invaders. It is said that they are a peaceful race that is older than Lemuria itself"

It did not look anything like you would see on an exploration channel on TV, or a science fiction movie. There were no huge lights illuminating the complex, nor a giant, clear glass dome allowing you to see the structures inside. Actually it looked more organic or natural.

There was indeed a dome, but it was a low profile, like only the top was sticking out of the ocean floor. It was covered in a thin layer of silt across the top, but none on the sides, indication the surface was smooth and slick. There were tunnels extending from the side that led to an underwater mountain. In fact, the dome was actually resting in a cavern between high rising cliffs. As the self guided sled took them on their approach run, the ride began to get a little turbulent, they were traveling over a field of rising bubbles and gasses from volcanic vents. They probably used the enormous heat to generate power for themselves. Finally, the sled dove toward the edge of one of the tunnels, and slipped into a small entrance. Mya was baffled; there was no gate, nor air lock of any kind, yet they had gone from the ocean, into a dry cave. How do they keep the water from rushing in?

Exiting their now dormant craft, Seth and Mya strained their vision to see where they were. There were no elaborate carvings or gilded ceilings, only dark, obsidian like walls. They could barely see anything, Mya was having a difficult time breathing, the air was very humid and dense, and the light traces of sulfur stung her eyes and nasal passages. Seth tugged on Mya's sleeve to get her attention; he was looking toward a corner of a tunnel connection. There, semi hiding in the entrance stood a child. Seth slowly kneeled on one knee, bringing him a little closer to the boy's height, he held out his long arm in a gesture of peace.

The small figure slowly emerged to greet them. Seth took the map with the symbol they were looking for and lay it on the ground to see if he recognized it. The boy took a few steps closer and squatted down to look. Seth pointed at it and asked,

"Do you know where this is? Have you seen this before?"

The little boy smiled and stood up, grabbing Seth's giant hand, pulling him to the tunnel. Mya grabbed up the map and followed behind them.

The tunnel entrance was large, but quickly shrunk in height. Seth hit his head more than once as he crouched down in order to keep moving, even Mya had to stoop over a bit. After a few uncomfortable moments, the trio emerged into a much larger room where they could stretch out their spines to a normal, upright position. In front of them was a large table and benches, although they were peculiarly low to the ground, odd plants of varying sizes, dotted the room. At the far end was a platform, which proudly supported an empty throne. Mya began studying her surroundings. There were no traditional lamps to speak of; the light came from large columns of bubbling water that encircled the room. She guessed that somehow, they were charging the gasses in the water causing them to glow. As they continued to look around, they realized the boy had left them alone.

Seth pointed out that the floor in front of the throne, had some type of map painted on it. He couldn't make out much of it unless he was looking at it from a higher per-spective, so he began climbing the steps up to the throne. Standing in front of the throne, he could see the elaborate detail of what looked to be a map of the ocean floor, show-ing great mountain ranges, deep caverns, and vast watery plains.

Mya wasn't even paying attention to what Seth was do-ing; she had made an astonishing discovery of her own. Along the walls and hung on shelves were remnants of nearly every civilization she could think of. Statuettes of Egyptian Pharos, small Indian canoes, jade carvings of Buddha, silver platters and gold coins hundreds of pots and masks from every civilization and corner of the globe. Some things she did not recognize, but then she saw some-thing that put a lump in her throat. Hanging proudly on a wall, a large piece of battered metal, pierced with silver dollar sized holes, a fading insignia with stripes and a star. A piece of history from her home, the remnant of a war-plane shot down into a watery grave.

"Are you here to take rule of my Kingdom?"

The silence had been broken by a man that had slipped

in unnoticed by both of them.

"You stand at my throne as though you have conquered me. Have I been?"

Seth scrambled down the steps.

"My deepest apology, I meant no disrespect, I was only trying to read the map."

Kneeling down to show respect and embarrassment, Seth asked forgiveness.

The man who questioned the takeover began chuckling and laughing loudly as Mya ran to Seth's side.

"Stand up, I only kid you. I know you are not here to threaten me"

He was a curious looking man, apparently a king or ruler of some sort, not a hair on his head, and wearing a simple smock. The two most peculiar features was his size, he couldn't have been more than five feet tall, and his skin, a dull grayish tone, and very oily looking, probably from a lack of sunlight. Taking a seat in the oversized throne, the jovial little man spoke.

"I am King Pel, who are you and what brings you to our city?"

"I am Seth, and this is Mya. We are Lemurian."

"Lemurian?" the King queried with a raised brow.

"I don't recall ever having Lemurian guests before, but I have heard stories of your people. I thought you would be taller." Pel broke into laughter again.

Mya laughed to herself, thinking 'I was taller than him when I was twelve'.

"When visitors come to my kingdom, they usually bring me gift from their homeland. Look around and all of the gifts on the walls that visitors have honored me with. What have you brought me?"

Mya thought he was cute at first, but his arrogance was

becoming annoying.

Looking through their backpacks, they both struggled to find something that would please him. Finally, Seth pulled out the snow globe he bought in Mt. Shasta and presented it to the King.

"This is where we are from, we live under the mountain."

Pel smiled as he took the gift from Seth.

"This will be a nice addition to my collection. Now, how can I help you?"

"The Travelers have stolen some valuable items from our Temple." Seth began to explain.

"They have our maps and guides to the portals, and we believe they have unlocked them all and are leaving them open."

Pel's expression quickly changed to concern.

"We were aware that something was wrong, we have seen a dramatic increase in the portal use, and we cannot close it either."

Mya pulled the map from her backpack.

"I have a map, and we believe we can close it behind us if you can show us where we can locate this symbol."

Pel studied the map and the symbol she was pointing to.

"I know where this is, the symbol is our city. If you can close it, I will show you to the portal. Leaving it unlocked is very dangerous. I do not know what the Travelers want, they have caused us no harm, but we should close the portal to be safe."

With that, Pel stood and began walking out of the room. Mya scrambled to fold her map and follow his lead. She desperately wanted to look at the artifacts in his collection, but there was no time for that, Seth was right on his heels and she needed to catch up. Always the reverent diplomat, Seth exclaimed.

"Your gracious assistance in most appreciated. We would enjoy seeing your kingdom on a return visit."

Pel moved very quickly for having such short stubby legs, Mya murmured to herself as she tried to catch them.

The labyrinth of tunnels was very confusing, but Seth and Mya stayed close behind Pel, until the reached an opening that led them to a large room with a small, raised platform in the center, carved on the center of the platform was the symbol they had been searching for. Pel stopped at the entrance.

"I have been here before, but have never used the portal, I do not know how, nor do I wish to. This has been here for thousands of years, built by others, to be used by others. I leave you now and wish you speed and wisdom."

And with that, the odd little king turned and left them.

It was very apparent to both of them that this room was identical to the room that Lemule was taken from, with exception to the symbol on the platform.

Upon closer examination of the platform, Mya noticed a depression in the center of the symbol. The depression matched the carved stone of her father's collection. They both decided that it must be the key to lock and unlock the portal, the problem was, they had no idea of where it would take them. Was there a way to control the destination?

One by one, they lowered the poles around the room with the crystals on top, careful to leave one up. Then, hand in hand, they lowered the last one, which made all six crystals focus a beam on the platform. Together they walked to the center, placed the key in the depression and turned it. Everything around them turned a brilliant blue in an instance, and then it simply faded, had it not worked? Did she turn the key the wrong direction? Their questions were quickly answered when they looked at the symbol below them. Although the room looked the same, the symbol was different from the one they were just at. This one Seth remembered as the one that Sinjin did not recognize on the map.

Mya pulled out her map and compared the symbols, she could not believe her eyes, the only place that symbol showed up on her map was in Antarctica! How could that be? They were just in the South Pacific, and in a matter of two seconds they were in Antarctica. Mya was fascinated with the idea of their instantaneous commute, but she had more pressing questions.

"There must be a way to control your destination with this thing, and we have to figure it out. Otherwise, we will be going wherever it wants to send us."

Seth removed the stone key from it's holding place and stepped off the platform and looked around the room.

"There is a tunnel over here!"

Mya joined him reluctantly; she was beginning to think this was turning into a goose chase. Seth yelled back from the tunnel, "There is a door here, it is locked. I don't think this place has been used in a while." Seth looked stumped.

"Maybe we should just close this portal and move on." He suggested.

"But to where?" Mya replied.

Seth thought about what Kira and Sinjin had both said to him. Turn to the Ancients and Nature, they will guide you. Mya had already spread the map out on the floor when Seth kneeled next to her.

"We must meditate, listen to the wisdom of those that wish to help us."

Mya had never been very good at meditating, she had tried a yoga class a few years ago and discovered that she could never relax enough, or clear her mind enough to be successful at it. She was a fidgeter. But she had changed a great deal since then, and was becoming more aware of her abilities. Seth had already slipped into his own world, Mya was trying too hard it seemed, but finally, she began to feel total peace and freedom to let go. Instead of forcing control of her thoughts and expectations, this time she simply waited for someone or something, to tell her what to do instead of her dictating a desired result. The feeling wasn't as foreign to her as she thought it would be. When she was trying to come up with ideas for her design customers, she subconsciously would receive impressions from her clients, allowing her to give them exactly what they were hoping for. One of the reasons she was so successful. As she sat silently in the dim room, hoping for some revelation, an image kept fading in and out of mind. It was one of the map symbols, a triangle with a spiral inside of it, along with the letter 'V' next to it. Mya assumed her mind was still focusing on the map she had been studying, and tried to force it from her conscience. Soon she began to lose focus and was thinking about everything from friends to food. She opened her eyes and started studying the map again. Glancing over at Seth, she realized his eyes were open also.

"You know, I have a gut feeling as to where we should go next."

"Me too," he replied.

Leaning over, Seth stretched out a finger and pointed on the map, "Here."

"That's exactly where I was thinking!" Mya exclaimed in surprise.

Her finger was now pointing at the same symbol. It was located somewhere in the southwestern part of the US.

"Well," Mya stated, "let's give it a try."

"I think if we both concentrate on the symbol, as we did in the sled, it may take us where we want."

Holding hands, they went back onto the platform, placed the key back into its slot, focused intensely on the symbol, and turned it. Once again the brilliant blue light surrounded them for a brief moment, then disappeared.

"It worked!" Mya yelled as she recognized the symbol below them.

"That's the one we were trying for."

Seth was pleased also, but not quite as enthusiastic as Mya.

"Let's go see why we were directed here."

Seth grabbed Mya's hand and pulled her toward the only exit from the room.

Chapter 18

Allison's eyes fluttered open, as if she had been in a long, deep sleep. The soft, glowing, fog that had enveloped and paralyzed her, had disappeared. Instead of looking at the peeled logs of the cabin's living room, she was now laying on the ground, in what seemed to be a cave, carved out of soft, red stone. She wondered if she was waking up from an all night party somewhere or what. Her mind seemed fuzzy, but suddenly, from behind her, a familiar voice called out.

"Allison? Allison? What on earth are you doing here?"

Allison scrambled to her feet, still a bit dazed, and certainly confused.

"Mya!"

The girls ran to each other and embraced so tightly they nearly squeezed the breath from one another.

Mya cupped her dear friend's face in her hands, she could see and sense the confusion Allison was dealing with.

"What are you doing here?" She asked again.

"I don't know. I was looking for you, and I went to Sinjin's cabin, next thing I know, I'm here."

"Why were you looking for me? What's wrong?"

Seth stood a ways behind Mya, not wanting to interrupt, but still very curious as to why Allison was there.

"Someone ransacked your apartment, I think they were looking for this."

Allison pulled the brass template from her pocket.

"You left it at my place, and I was worried for you. So, I looked up Sinjin, and he told me that you needed this, and someone was trying to keep you from having it. Next thing I know, I'm here."

"You poor dear, are you alright?"

"I think so. Where are we?"

Grabbing her hand and leading her out of the cave, Mya suggested they find out.

Walking out into the bright sunlight was a challenge for Seth and Mya, they had been in dark tunnels and under the ground for what seemed like an eternity.

They both raised their arms to shade their sensitive eyes, but their skin drank in the warmth of the sun. Mya had been so immersed in her new quest, and newly discovered ancestry; she didn't realize how much she missed her own world.

Standing outside the cave, the trio surveyed the landscape they had been placed in. A few trees, large red rock outcroppings and a few mountains. As they walked down the mountain, Mya could feel rushes of energy blowing upwards from the ground, as if she were passing over steam grates in a city. A few yards later, a blast of energy would rush down from the sky into the ground. She looked back to see if Seth or Allison had noticed anything, but it appeared they did not.

About thirty minutes into their descent, they heard a noise from around the bend, soon the saw a tour jeep making it's way around the bend.

"Okay Seth, we are in my world now, watch me work."

Mya said in a sarcastic tone. Waiving her arms to get the driver's attention, Mya was about to put her charm to work. As the jeep got closer, she made out the placard on the side of the door, 'Mystical Tours of Sedona' in bold letters under a painted rainbow.

Looking over her shoulder, she announced, "We're in Arizona guys." Allison looked surprised; Seth had no concept as to where that was.

"Hi, you folks lost?" the driver asked.

"Actually we probably are. But more importantly, my friend isn't feeling well. Is there any way we could get a lift back to town?"

Mya's flirting was in high gear.

Without hesitation, the driver said yes. Although rather bouncy, the jeep ride was a welcome relief from their walking. Mya sat in the front with the driver, continuing to flirt with him and making casual conversation.

"So why are you out here with no tourists? Just taking a joyride?"

"Actually, my boss got a call from the park service about some people camping up here, which is not allowed. I didn't see anyone, must have been some kids partying."

"Well, we didn't see anyone else either." Added Mya.

Seth sat in the back next to Allison, grinning broadly.

"Good to see you again." He said.

Allison just put on a half smile in response; she still was unsure of this guy, and a little confused with what had just happened.

"If you could drop us off over there, that would be

great." Mya pointed to a corner with a small motel. They all piled out as he pulled the jeep along side the curb. Mya leaned back in and gave the surprised diver an appreciative kiss on the cheek.

"Well, I hope your friend feels better, be careful."

Waving, he pulled away, grateful for the kiss, but was hoping for her phone number.

"Seth, do you still have that envelope full of money?" Mya asked.

"I have my credit cards, but if someone is trying to find us, it will be more difficult if we only use cash."

Seth dug through his pack, withdrew the folded up envelope, and handed it to Mya.

"I wish I could find a man like that." Allison joked.

"Come on guys, let's get a room, I could really use a shower."

The desk clerk smiled oddly when Mya asked for one room for all three of them, but nothing really surprised her anymore, she thought she had seen it all. The only room available had a king-size bed, so they would have to share it, but at least it was a bed.

Allison finally had an opportunity to quiz Mya.

"Okay, now you know I respect and trust you dearly, but have to tell me what's going on and where you have been, especially now that I got dragged into this."

She was not about to let her friend off the hook easily.

"I'm so sorry you got caught up in this, it's so difficult to explain, but you do deserve some answers." Mya responded, giving her best friend a much-needed hug.

"First of all, I don't know a lot of the answers, I'm still trying to figure out many things myself. I have learned to keep an open mind about more things, and accept some pretty weird stuff. Second, everything Seth told us before is true."

"What about this Sinjin guy? I only spoke to him briefly, he said he was going to try and reach you, then WHAM, I'm laying in a cave with you standing over me."

"You're not going to believe this, but, Sinjin is my Grandfather, my Dad's Dad. Apparently, I have the same gift they did, a high sensitivity to certain types of energy fields. That's why I was feeling so strange recently. Anyway, Seth's village was robbed of some maps and sacred items, that they think I can locate for them."

Allison just looked at Mya as if she didn't know whether Mya had lost her mind, or to trust her. "I'm going to take a shower, then we should get some fresh clothes for us, and then get something to eat. You know what I'm dying for? A hot, pepperoni pizza, with extra cheese. How about you guys?"

"Sounds yummy to me." Allison cheerfully agreed.

"What is a pizza?" Seth asked.

The pounding streams of hot water from the shower felt so good as the droplets massaged her neck and head. Mya's mind wandered as she tried to recall all that she had been through, and what their next move should be to accomplish their goals for the villagers. After putting a robe on, and tucking her wet hair into a makeshift turban, she walked out to the balcony to join Seth. The desert landscape enchanted him; it was so vast, so beautiful. Allison had hopped into the shower while the other two watched the people walk through the souvenir shops.

After several minutes, Allison emerged from the bathroom, expecting to find them on the balcony still, but instead was shocked to see Mya laying naked on the bed, and Seth rubbing oil on her.

"Whoa! I'm sorry, I didn't know." Allison blurted out and turned to go back in the bathroom.

"No! It's okay; it's not like that. This is protective oil that Seth is putting on me. I had some before, but it washed off in the shower. Really, it's fine, come back here." Mya reassured her friend there was nothing sexual going on; Allison wasn't totally convinced.

"Hey, I found a place to go as soon as you are ready. It's called the 'Pizza Palace' and it's just down the street. I'm starved."

Chapter 19

Seth stood at the large pane glass window, watching the cook toss and knead the dough for their dinner. He was amazed that the cook could spin and toss it that high into the air without dropping it. The girls had settled into a booth and were enjoying a few glasses of wine. Seth had moved into the arcade and watched several kids playing video games. The bells and buzzers were loud and mesmerizing. He figured out they were playing some sort of game, since they were laughing. He was tempted to try one himself, but he did not understand what he was to do, so he watched instead. His concentration was broken when he heard a voice shouting from the arcade door.

"Hey tall guy! Pizza's ready."

It was Allison, waving him back to their table.

Seth struggled for a way to hold the flimsy triangle, while the girls stuffed their mouths. Finally, success, with his fingers grasping the crust, and his long thumb supporting the middle, he jambed the gooey mixture of cheese, pepperoni and bread into his mouth. It was wonderful, he thought.

"I wonder if I could make this back home?"

Seth asked.

"I could see it now, 'Seth's Pizza Place'."

Mya laughed with the others. Seth's laughter stopped momentarily when he glanced down and watched all the toppings slide off his piece. Leaving a sad looking, droopy red slice of dough in his hand.

"Ahhhh." The girls choired, and then continued their giggling.

Undeterred, Seth piled the glob back onto his slice as neatly as possible and took another bite. Allison and Mya couldn't eat another piece, Seth had already downed six pieces, he loved it. They asked for a box to take the remaining pizza back to the room. They were all in a pretty good mood, the most relaxed in a long time.

On their walk home, Allison stopped into a liquor store and bought some more White Zinfendel.

"Seth, do you have a favorite libation?" She asked.

"I don't think he drinks." Mya interupted.

"We drink wine too, but it does not have all those funny names that you use."

It was pretty late by the time they reached the motel; no one was out, except a few passerby's.

"Why is there a small lake here?" Seth asked.

"It's not a lake dear, but we could sit next to it and finish our wine." Mya suggested. All three took off their sandals and shoes to dangle their aching, tired feet. In mid conversation, Allison looked over at Mya with a devilish grin.

"Are you thinking what I'm thinking?"

"Uh huh." Twisting her neck around looking for others

and seeing the 'coast was clear' Mya shouted in a loud whisper, "Skinny dipping!"

Without missing a beat, both girls stripped and dove into the cool water. Seth remained at the pool's edge, not surprised by their nakedness, but still hesitating to join them.

"Come on you big chicken." Allison taunted him.

"I do not know how to swim very well." He announced.

"Oh; well, we will teach you then. Now get those clothes off and get in." Allison barked. Nervously, the long legged giant slipped into the cool water. Standing in the shallow end, he had to crouch down substantially to get his head under. When he stood up, Allison gasped and stared without shame. His long wet hair was slicked back and cascaded over his broad shoulders like a mane, water dribbled down his chest over his well defined abs back into the pool. He was so tall, the water level covered just below his navel. He looked like a model in a magazine ad. Her trance was broken by Mya splashing water at her. Allison swam over to her.

"Would you look at that body! He's a hunk."

Mya just laughed.

"Okay Seth, let's start by learning to kick, grab onto the edge like this."

Soon all three of them were stretched out, kicking their legs in unison.

"I think he has the hang of that. Allison, swim to the other side. Seth, watch how she uses her arms to stay afloat and pull herself through the water."

Allison shot off across the pool like a pro, hardly making a splash, reaching the other side she made a sloppy turn and returned.

"Your turn Seth, come here."

Seth waded over to Mya nervously.

"I'll hold your hands and keep your head out of the water, Allison will hold your hips up in the water while you kick."

Mya knew she was torturing Allison, and smirked at her friend. Allison was in heaven, or was it a teasing hell? Here she was, a little buzzed, totally nude, under the moon, cradling the naked pelvis of this lean Adonis, while he tried kicking his long legs. She looked over at Mya, standing in front of him, and holding his outstretched hands giving him encouragement. Catching her eye, Allison motioned with her head for Mya to look at his small, glistening butt floating at her own chest. Jokingly, Allison bit her bottom lip, indicating restraint.

"I think I am ready to try now." Seth announced.

"Lets start at the edge here," Mya directed.

"This way you can push off the side. Swim to Allison over there, she will grab you and pull you up. Remember, don't panic, and don't stop kicking until you reach her."

Though a little nervous, Seth drew in a big breath, held it and pushed off towards his target. His legs were kicking madly, and his arms were flailing and splashing like a wounded animal. Allison rushed toward him, trying to see through the splashing and trying not to get nailed by his long arms. Gasping for air as Allison pulled him up by his arm pits, Seth grinned at her.

"Did I swim? Did I?"

"Very good first time." Mya praised, she didn't want to burst his excitement by telling him he only went about five feet.

"Let's try again, this time try to relax your arms and not splash so much."

Seth kept improving as Allison kept backing up, making him swim further.

After the lesson, the playful girls tried to tackle and dunk Seth, Mya hugged his thigh, in an attempt to uproot him, while Allison clung to his back, her legs wrapped around his waist, and her arms over his shoulders, hanging on his chest. The sexual tension was almost too great for all of them, especially Allison, who was enjoying having her wet, naked breasts pressed against Seth's muscular back.

"Alright you guys, out of the pool. This isn't that kind of motel."

The mood was broken, as the desk clerk had come out to put an end to their frolicking.

"I should have know it was you three." She said, recalling when they checked in.

"It's not that I'm opposed to it, hell, I'd join you if I could. But we have families staying here."

"Oh, sorry, we just about to get out anyway," Mya answered.

They hadn't any towels, so they gathered up their clothing and streaked to the room. The fun was over, much to the dismay of a few guests enjoying the show from their windows.

Collapsing in a giggling heap on the bed, Allison was changing her mind about having to share it, maybe not such a bad thing after all, she thought.

"I haven't had that much fun in while," Mya said. "But tomorrow, we need to get some more clothes and food. I also want to find a library, I have an idea."

Exhausted from the water play, the still nude trio slipped under the covers; girl, boy, girl, to get some sleep. Before long, Mya and Seth were fast asleep, but Allison couldn't doze off, her mind still in a sexual frenzy. It was like one of her fantasies about to come true. Laying in a warm bed, with nothing on, and a man with a lean, chiseled body squeezed right up next to her. She turned on her side, laying right up next to him, she desperately tried to keep her heavy breathing quiet. Allison wrestled with the temptation to slide her trembling hand across that rippled stomach. Not quite sure what was truly going on between him and Mya, she reluctantly pulled her hand back to herself in frustration. It was going to be a long night she thought.

Chapter 20

Allison awoke first, to find an arm draped over her and a warm body pressed next to her. Hoping it was Seth, her excitement faded when she saw the thin arm was Mya's.

"It was cold, and you were warm." Mya explained.

"Where is Seth?" Allison asked as she sat up. Glancing around the room, they saw him stretched out on the floor.

"The bed must have been too soft for him."

Once everybody was up and dressed, they headed out, stopping briefly at the lobby for complimentary fruit and bagels. Seth grabbed a few extras for his backpack.

"The desk clerk told me the library is only a few blocks away. I'll explain what I'm looking for as we walk."

Mya, it seemed, had a plan.

Once inside the library, Mya headed straight for a computer terminal. Seth was awestruck by the amount of books on the shelves, and was walking through the building very cautiously; Allison went back and grabbed him by the hand, leading him like a child.

"Should we be in here?" A curious Seth asked Mya.

"Is this not a sacred place with all of these writings?"

"No." Mya replied, trying to make a point, in defense of her civilization.

"We do not hide our books and knowledge from the people. Everyone is able to come here and learn whatever they wish."

Trying to understand the openness of their society, Seth asked,

"So, anyone in the city, can come here, and learn from all of this knowledge in these many writings, without special permission?"

Feeling confident that she had proved her point, Mya answered

"Yes, it's true. It is open to all."

Pausing for a moment to think, Seth asked with a curious face.

"Then why are there so few people here? It would seem that this place would be crowded with people wanting to learn."

Touché, Seth had made a stronger point than she had. Here was all the information and entertainment most people should ever need; yet the truth was, the massive volumes of knowledge and answers, were taken for granted. Most people, had become numbed by too much television and movies; bubble gum for the brain, someone once said.

"Well Seth, you're right about that, this place should be crowded."

Mya had been searching the internet for sites that contained information on the earth's magnetic fields. There were hundreds of returns from her search, so she narrowed it down, typing 'MAGNETIC IMAGES'. While the search engine did it's thing, Seth asked what it was doing.

"The computer is looking all over the internet, for documents related to what we ask for."

"What is the internet?" He asked innocently.

How do you explain the internet? She thought.

"Hmm, okay, here is an analogy. You know the cosmic knowledge you keep talking about? Or the Knowledge Crystal? It's like that. By accessing the internet, you can find the answers to almost anything you can think of."

Seth was amazed and a bit shocked.

"And I suppose anyone can talk with the internet also?"

"Yes, anyone."

"That sounds very dangerous." Seth said sadly.

The results were still disappointing, as there were 537 matches, most of them related to medical sites and MRI's. Mya scrolled through the unrelated pages, looking for any hints of magnetic images of the earth, when suddenly a word scrolled past the screen. Scrolling back up the page, the words satellite images, appeared.

"Here we go, that's what we need."

Allison leaned over from her terminal to see what she had found.

A non-official website, that showed images of the magnetic fields of the planet. The images, taken by a Japanese owned satellite, were used to try and predict deadly earthquakes, by monitoring the fluctuations of the magnetic rings around the earth.

The satellite took images twice daily, and updated the site automatically. The site was fascinating to Mya, looking at the hit counter, she could tell she was one of only a few. The other hits were probably the site owners, or some engineering nerd surfing from his dorm.

"Help me look for any changes in the fields as we compare images day by day, and write them down."

The site was actually pretty well done, you could even zoom into a fairly small geographic area.

Since all three of them had been 'sent' here, one way or another, maybe they should focus on Arizona. The images of the radiation were like a puzzle, the problem was, even if they had all the pieces, what where they looking for? Mya had gone back seven days worth of images of Arizona, aside from an occasional spike, there seemed little change in the lines and rings. It looked similar to a topographical map.

Progressing closer to the most recent images, Allison noticed a slight shift in color and shape of one of the bands. When the next image loaded, the change was much more obvious, it was forming a new pattern, and with each update, a more distinct design was appearing. Seth pointed at the screen.

"This looks similar to a symbol I have seen, but it is not complete."

Mya hit the 'next' button to display the image next in line.

"They should get a DSL for this slow piece of junk." Allison scoured.

Slowly as the most current image loaded, they could see what they had predicted. The magnetic radiation, escaping the earth, was forming two new patterns, both were symbols from Mya's map, and a third was developing. The last image was taken eleven hours ago, that meant there was only one hour before the next image was available.

"Quick, print out a copy of it and compare those symbols with the ones on the map." Ordered Mya.

Taking the print, they moved to a large table and un-

Darin Williams

folded the map Mya's father had drawn. As they surveyed the map, Allison went to retrieve a local map, to see where they needed to go.

Mya already knew; they had to go back up the hill they just came down from. She recalled the bursts of energy she had felt under her feet as the navigated the rocky trail. Seth pointed out the two symbols on the map matched the two from the satellite image, but the satellite image showed a third symbol forming. There was no third image on her map.

"Okay, it's been about an hour, let's go see if the next image is ready."

Mya gasped when she turned to walk back to the computer, there was a kid sitting at it. They should have stayed with it. Looking around for another free terminal, all she could see was a few vacant ones with 'out of order' signs taped to them. Time seemed to move so much slower as they waited for someone to finish. Mya expressed her concern to Allison.

"If this variation in magnetic resonance triggers some type of gateway that we need, we better not miss it; who knows when it will do it again?"

After what seemed like an eternity, the boy that had taken over their terminal got up and left. Mya made a mad dash to secure it, as if it was the last lottery ticket.

Mya's fingers typed in the site's URL as fast as they could, and then waited for the page to display. Finally the opening page loaded completely, now she just had to scroll to the button that would display the latest image taken, then set the parameters of their geographic search, and hit enter.

"Please work, please work." Allison murmured.

Line by line, slowly the image loaded, until the third symbol was as clear as the others.

126

"Look! There it is, hurry and print it out before this dinosaur locks up."

Once the print came out, Allison shouted to Mya, "Got it!"

Mya quickly shut down the computer and grabbed her pack.

Walking back to the motel, they made a quick stop into a convenience store for water, power bars and other snacks, then headed back down the road.

"Hey," Allison pointed out, "isn't that the tour company we rode with the other day?"

Mya agreed. "Let's see if we can get a ride back up."

Mya was very pleased to see the young man that gave them a ride, was behind the counter. His eyes lit up when she walked in.

"Hi, remember us?" she said coyly.

"Sure, how could I forget?" He replied, in an attempt to flirt.

"Is your friend feeling better?" He asked.

"Oh, much better, thanks. Hey, we need a ride back up the hill now, think we can hire you?"

"Well, there is another tour leaving in two hours, want to sign up?"

"Actually, we need to go now, and since you know where you picked us up, I was hoping you could drive." Mya asked.

"I wish I could, but there's no one here to cover the desk."

Tired of playing the game, Mya said.

"Look, I'll pay you three hundred bucks if you take us right now."

Considering that was three times what he would normally get, he replied, "I'll leave a note."

Driving up the rocky trail at a speed that was barely

safe, Allison gladly held onto Seth and they tried not to bounce out of the jeep, he didn't seem to mind. Mya would give the driver a few directions, leading them to the drop off point.

"Not too many people come to this area, most go to the usual places, over that way. That's where a lot of groups have their get-togethers and such."

"We don't care for the crowded trails." Mya commented.

Mya was noticing a big change in the energy around her as they neared the place they had been picked up.

"Here would be good."

She didn't want him to see where the cave was that they had been in. The jeep came to a halt, sliding a few feet in the loose dirt. The passengers all climbed out.

"You guys be careful now, when the sun goes down it can get pretty chilly up here."

"Thank you, we'll be fine." Shouted Mya.

The sound of the jeep began to fade out as they continued their ascent.

The surges of energy coming from the ground were now pulsing powerfully through Mya's body.

"Are you sure you don't feel anything at all?" She said, turning back to Seth.

"No, I don't."

The late afternoon sun scraped the inner walls of they cave, they had found themselves in a few days ago. Mya led them to the back wall where the hidden staircase led to the portal that brought them here.

"Guys?" Allison said, "This might be normal for you, but it's new to me, could you slow down a bit?"

Everything was the same as when they left it, all six crystal topped poles were pointing at each other, the familiar shafts of light focused on the platform. One thing Seth did notice, was that on the other side of the room was a small niche carved in the wall, as he got closer, he could see the two symbols they saw on the map.

"Only the first symbol was here before, look around for the third." Seth instructed.

Mya had her map out, and the satellite image next to it.

"It has to be hear somewhere, keep looking."

The energy fields were so strong now, Mya was having a difficult time concentrating. How could it feel so strong to her, yet Seth acted as though nothing had changed.

Allison had made her way to the other side of the room to look at what Seth had found. A puzzled look came over her face.

"Wait a minute. Now I remember where I had seen those symbols before."

Reaching into her back pocket,

"It's on your bookmark!" she exclaimed as she held up the brass template that got her involved in the beginning. Mya gathered up her papers and scrambled over to see. Seth took the template and held it over the raised symbols, matching them up, it slipped right in place.

"But what about the missing symbol?"

"Look, when in place, the template points to the top of the niche, there is a hole up there." Explained Mya.

"So the last symbol must be portable."

Seth suddenly remembered something.

"Mya, take out your father's stones."

Emptying her belongings onto the ground, Mya opened the pouch holding his collection. Spreading the assortment out, Seth stretched out a finger and pointed to the szja,

"It's in here, the symbol is carved on the stone your father placed in here. You must open it."

Mya had tried and failed many times to open the box. But she had never been so focused in her life. She had to succeed this time. Mya once more, picked up the box, found the stone on the bottom with her thumb, and began to concentrate. The rhythmic waves of intense, magnetic pulses distracted her terribly, she had to completely clear her mind, and match the frequency of the stone that sealed the box, just as Seth had taught her. Without realizing, the edges of the box slid open.

"You did it Mya! You have mastered it."
Seth said proudly.

There was little celebration on Mya's part, she reached inside, and laying next to her childhood photograph, was the stone, carved with the symbol they had been searching for. Mya took the stone, kissed it for good luck, and pressed it into place. A slow rumble began to vibrate under their feet as the platform in the center of the room began sinking, lowering itself until it dropped below floor level, exposing a stairway. Looking at each other for consensus, they all agreed to go.

Chapter 21

Mya retrieved the stone and the template before heading down the stairs. There was another niche on the side of the staircase with the same symbols, Seth suggested it was to close the entrance behind them, they agreed to try it. With the template in place, and the stone pressed in it's holder, the platform ground its way back into position. A very nervous Allison worried if they had just sealed their own tomb. They had been walking through the narrow tunnel for only a short time, when they emerged into a very large cavern, there were no altars, or drawings of any kind, just a large rocky floor and a huge ceiling. As they explored the cave, Allison made an announcement.

"Does the floor feel like it's moving to anyone else, or is it just me?"

Seth and Mya stopped walking to see if they could tell.

"It does feel like that, but not like an earthquake kind of thing." Mya agreed.

Allison walked carefully over to Mya for comfort, Seth

had walked a little further into the cave,

"Water," he shouted. "There is a lake over here."

The girls gingerly walked over to see.

"Actually," he added, "I think we are floating on it."

"This is rock we are standing on Seth, rock doesn't float." Allison said, pointing out the obvious. In a very serious tone, Seth knelt down by the water's edge.

"This one does, watch."

The girls looked on as Seth took a rock the size of a grapefruit, and set it on the water. To their amazement, it didn't sink, in fact it rested right on top of the surface with just a few bubbles churning underneath it.

Seth tried pushing it under, as he did, the water became more turbulent around the curious rock. The water seemed to be repelling the rock. Seth was enjoying his little experiment, as was evident from his grin. Taking the rock from the water, he stood up and said,

"Watch this."

Seth lowered his arm, and then pitched the rock in a high, under armed lob. The rock hit the water with a splash, and disappeared under the surface. Seth looked at the girls in disbelief, when suddenly a large woosh and geyser of water sent the rock back into the air, this time it settled back on the surface. Seth's grin returned.

Allison piped up, "What the hell kind of rock is this?"

In a hushed voice, and the smile of child he whispered,.

"The FireStone."

Mya's ears perked up at that,.

"Kira told us to bring this back, grab some pieces and put them in your packs." She instructed.

The cavern had obviously been mined at some point, you could see gouges in the walls, made by some type of instrument. Seth had wandered off to another section of the cave and discovered a long wooden pole leaning against a wall. As he reached for it, he realized the ground he was standing on was either a separate piece or a section that had been broken off. Seth called the girls over.

"Hop on, let's see where this lake goes to."

The cavern was dimly lit, but their eyes had adjusted enough to see some detail. Mya was not too worried, as she knew that Seth's vision was very acute in the dark. Even so, she had brought a halogen flashlight along, one of the items she picked up at the convenience store.

Seth grabbed the pole and pushed it against the wall to cast them off. The small, floating island moved gently from its dock, but then moved right back into place. After another attempt, with the same results, it was apparent that the stony bout would only travel in one direction, which is why it didn't float away on it's own. Using the pole and their hands, they pushed and rotated the little island around, until it pointed to the open lake, then with a final push with the pole, they were sent gliding into the waters. The speed was not great, but consistant and the ride was amazingly smooth, no sound came from underneath, not even the sound of water splashing out of the way. It was almost as if they were skimming above the surface.

"Where do you think this takes us? What if there is a waterfall at the end of this?" Allison was not quite the adventurer that Mya was.

"I don't think there is a waterfall, if there was, you could hear it in this echo chamber."

As they drifted at a leisurely pace through the cavern, they could make out various letters and markings on the walls. The markings were not elaborate or anything seen in the Temples or portals, these were almost graffiti like, as if to say 'John was here'. How old were these, were they recent? They all wondered.

The cavern was narrowing, barely three feet on either

side of their floating rock. Eventually, their cruise ended when the ceiling of the tunnel, which had been tapering downward, came so low to the water's surface, they could go no further.

"Hey, at least we made it this far," Mya said as she stood up. "We might as well let everyone know we did."

She drew a pocket knife from her pack and scrawled on the wall along side some other traveler's mark, 'Seth, Allison and Mya 2K8'

"2K8? What is that?" Seth asked.

"The year we were here," Mya explained, as she stuffed the knife back in her pack, "2008"

"Well, where to now Huck?" Allison asked. "It looks like a dead end to me." Allison was in a hurry to get back to the surface. Seth had a bewildered look on his face, and then suddenly piped in.

"Are you referring to Huck Finn?"

Mya and Allison looked at each other is surprise.

"How do you know about him?" Mya asked.

"Oh, I have read about him in my studies, he was a very adventurous person."

Seth fancied himself a Huckelberry Finn, a curious mind and adventurous soul. Allison and Mya were amazed that he would have even had access to such books from their world.

"One thing that I have found out," Mya explained, "There is no such thing as a dead end."

With the aid of the flashlight, they searched the cave's walls and ceiling for any clues or markings that would indicate another route.

"Shine the light down here," Seth directed, he was on his hands and knees looking where the cave walls met the water.

"Some of the carvings left by others, go below the surface of the water. That means the water level changes at some time."

Now all three of them were trying to look into the water for more clues.

"I see it," shouted Allison. "It's the same symbols on the template."

A thin groove pointed directly to a niche, identical to the one that brought them to the cave, the only problem was that it was two feet under water and tucked slightly behind a ledge out of reach.

"There's no way to get to it. I wonder if we have to wait for a tide cycle or something?" Asked Mya.

"What if there isn't, or if it happens every two years?" Allison added.

"I can reach it." Said Seth.

Seth certainly had the longest arms, but this looked even too far for him.

"Let me try, hand me the template."

Mya had all the confidence in the world in Seth, but was still apprehensive about the reach. Laying on his stomach, Seth crawled to the edge of their rocky raft, and stretched his long arm into the water. Feeling his way along the groove that disappeared under the water's surface to the niche, Seth could only extend his index finger as the other fingers clutched the template. As his hand got closer to the niche, the depression it was in, recessed behind the ledge just inches out of his reach.

Seth squirmed and scooted closer to the edge, to the point where he could feel the symbols that the template would slip over. Struggling to position the now slippery piece of metal over the rocky protrusions proved more difficult than it looked. Seth's arm muscles were fatigued from being stuck in the same position for so long, and in the water. He eventually realized that he had the template reversed in his hand, and tried to flip it around with his fingertips.

"I almost have it in place." An exhausted Seth announced as his extended digits strained to seat the metal plate."

Allison leaned over Mya's shoulder to see how close he was, but when she put her hand on the wall to get a better view, she inadvertently pushed the raft away from the wall, causing Seth to plunge into the water and lose hold of the template.

"Seth!" Mya yelled.

Fortunately, he had reached back with his other hand, and grabbed the edge of the raft as his slipped into the water. Mya and Allison grabbed him under the arms and by his waistband to drag him up.

"I'm so sorry, I'm so sorry," Allison said in a panic.

"Are you alright?"

"Yes, I'm fine, but I dropped the template."

Mya scrambled for the flashlight and franticly searched below the surface.

Fortunately, it was lying on the ledge right below the niche, unfortunately, it was now nearly a foot lower than before, now how would they reach it? After resting a short while, Seth went back to the waters' edge and tried to figure out how to get the template back. Even if there were no other passages, they needed it back to get out the way they came in.

"I have an idea." He said.

Picking up the pole, Seth stretched it across the water and rested the other end on a small rocky crag near his target.

"Hold this end in place so it doesn't roll."

Seth held onto the pole as he slipped back into the water. The girls were concerned because they knew Seth was not too good a swimmer, but he was already in the water, shuffling his hands along the pole, pulling him closer to his goal. Once he had positioned himself over the niche, Seth only needed to reach down and retrieve the template and slip it into place, which he did easily.

"It's on." He shouted. "Now I just need to place the stone above it."

Cradling the pole under his arm, Seth pulled the stone from his pocket and pressed it into the hole that it was carved for. Everyone held their breath waiting for something to happen, but nothing did. Had they gone through all this for nothing? Seth was still hanging onto the pole when he noticed that it was slowly beginning to angle and was about to dislodge from the wall. He quickly pulled the metal template and stone from the wall before it was unreachable. The pole fell and the girls were now pulling it back to them with Seth holding on and kicking his legs to help; he looked like hooked fish flailing. Once onboard, Mya quickly put the stone and template back in her pack so they would not fall back in the water.

The niche that Seth had struggled so hard to reach, was now at eye level along with many other carvings that had been hidden below the surface. As the level of the water continued to lower, an opening began to appear in the wall in front of them, growing in size as the water drained below them. Suddenly, a huge blast of mist belched out of the hole hitting them all in the face. Then a loud continuous roar could be heard from inside, and their rocky raft began to be sucked inside with great speed. The three of them huddled close to the ground and held onto one another, hoping not to get tossed off.

"It sounds like a waterfall, you told me there wasn't a waterfall!" Allison yelled.

Chapter 22

The sound was deafening and the ride was bumpy; it was like running a whitewater rapids in the dark. Finally, after what felt like twenty minutes, the churning water spit them out of the unlit tunnel onto a smooth quiet river. Mya looked at everyone to make sure no one was hurt, Allison looked like a scared cat that just experienced it's first swim, Seth sat quietly, trying not to let on how nervous he had been. Everyone was in tact, and no one had lost their bags.

With the sound of the thunderous waters fading behind them, they studied their new surroundings. They were now floating lazily down a calm river, flanked by enormous trees and plants the size of giant redwoods. The foliage was thick and so dense, you could not see the canopy or even the sky. A heavy mist shrouded everything and the heat made it feel like a sauna.

"It looks like the Amazon." Mya noted.

"We were just in Arizona a half hour ago Mya."

Allison pointed out.

"I don't think we are actually on the Amazon, it just looks like it." Mya added.

Tall reeds and grasses lined both sides of the river, making it impossible to get to land.

"I'll keep going until I see a break in the bank so we can get off." Announced Seth as he continued to steer them with the pole.

"As long as this doesn't lead to another waterfall, otherwise I'm swimming for shore." Quipped Allison. "I wonder if there are piranhas in there?"

Mya was becoming more worried about her friend, she shouldn't have even been in this situation, but also knew that she would have done the same thing if Allison was in her spot. Before things to too crazy, they ought to figure out a way to get Allison back home.

"I see a spot to land over there." Said Seth as he pointed out a small cove with an undersized strip of sand in front.

Pushing the pole off of the bottom of the river, Seth managed to redirect the self -propelled raft. To everyone's surprise, he guided it onto the petite beach head like a seasoned riverboat pilot. Seth wedged their slow moving rock next to a tree trunk and then drove the pole into the river bottom on the opposite side, effectively pinning their ride in place.

"Nice work." Remarked an impressed Allison. "You really are a Huck Finn."

Seth beamed with pride from the comparison.

"Okay you two, grab your bags and let's see where we are." Directed Mya.

Trudging through the tangle of vines and tall grass was no easy task, especially while breathing the hot and humid air. Mya led the way while a quickly fading Allison tried to keep up, Seth was in the rear, not paying attention to where they were going, but silently memorizing every step they had taken. Without his incredible memory, they wouldn't have a chance of finding their way back to the raft.

"Guys, I'm sorry, but I have to take a break before I pass out." Pleaded Allison.

"That's okay, we all should sit down for a bit." Agreed Mya.

Allison's face was flush and her breathing was labored. All three of them were drenched in sweat, their clothes clung heavily on them.

"I hope no one minds, but this shirt has to come off." Allison said, as she pulled her soaked shirt off of her back, revealing a thin, light blue sports bra that resembled sexy lingerie more than athletic support. Not wanting to make her friend feel as though she was the only one affected by the humidity, Mya stripped her shirt off also.

"Good idea." She added, now standing in a sports bra as well.

"Hey!" Allison barked, pointing her finger at Mya.

"Isn't that bra one that I let you borrow? Like six months ago?"

Looking down at her own chest, then back at her friend, Mya could only say "Oops."

They both began laughing like schoolgirls. Feeling a bit left out, Seth pulled his shirt off also. Allison seemed to perk up a little more after that, especially when he began fanning her with the map. While the fanning seemed to cool her off a little, Seth could tell that Allison's energy was still very low, so he put the map down and placed his hands on either side of her neck, pressing his fingers into the depressions just behind the ears. Gently massaging those two points for a few seconds, Seth slowly slid his huge hands over her shoulders, down her glistening arms, until her petite hands were swallowed up in his. Her widened eyes were fixed on her Adonis until he gently closed his eyes and concentrated on transferring some of his energy to her. She had never experienced such an overwhelming, intense feeling in her life. A steady, pulsating series of waves flooded her body, from her hands, up her arms and neck, reaching the crown of her head and then down her body, all the way to her toes. Her whole body was pulsating from the inside out, she felt as if she might explode. Mya fully understood what was going on, and decided to look for some fruit while Seth tried to re-energize her friend. After what felt like fifteen minutes, Seth released her hands, and waited for her to open her eyes.

"I hope that helps." Seth said.

Allison nodded her head and replied, "Oh yeah."

"Anyone hungry?"

Mya's voice pierced the air.

"Look what I found, mangos."

Seth quickly went to help her carry the armload of fruit. Allison stood up, a little unsure if her legs would steady her; they felt like noodles.

As Seth peeled the tropical fruit, Mya asked her friend.

"Are you feeling better? Do you have more energy?"

Allison grabbed her by the arm and whispered in her ear.

"Oh…my…gawd. You have no idea!"

Mya kissed her on the cheek and gave her a sneaky little smile and replied.

"Oh yes I do…"

Allison just covered her open mouth in surprise and giggled.

The fresh mango, along with the rest period seemed to have helped them all, but the infusion of energy that Seth gave Allison, which she still didn't quite understand, really did the trick. She had a lot of spring in her step, and had become much more enthusiastic, which bolstered Mya's spirit.

"Maybe we should look for a hill so we can see what's around us." Allison suggested.

"Do we even know what we are looking for?"

"No." Replied Mya. "I'm not even sure where we are; but it does look like the jungle is thinning, as soon as we can get out from under these dripping trees we will check our map for any clues."

The ever present haze had not let up at all. The large tropical plants collected the mist on their broad leaves until it rolled off in streams on their heads. The foliage was indeed thinning out, and eventually, they broke out into what appeared to be a deliberate clearing. Although the ground still had plants growing on it, remnants of old paths could be made out. Unsure of where the paths would take them, or how long they were, Mya pulled out her map and spread it in front of them.

"Okay, here is the last symbol we saw." Pointing to the symbol that matched the template.

"Yes, but it only shows up once on the map. We saw it three times. Once in the cave that I woke up in, again when we closed that entrance, and a third time in the water. Which one is represented on the map?"

Allison brought up a valid point, with only one symbol marked on the map, they couldn't even be sure which direction they had traveled.

"As much as I hate to mark up my father's papers, I think I should at least add two more symbols next to this one."

Studying the map for any clue to where they might be, the girls had not noticed that Seth had ventured a little further down the path; until he called back to them.

"Maybe this will help."

Allison and Mya looked up to see what he was talking about.

"What is it?" Mya replied. They saw nothing but the path fading into the dense fog.

"You wanted a mountain? I have found one for you." Seth shouted back.

The girls gathered the map and bags, and scurried up the path next to Seth to see what his outstretched arm was pointed at. As they came along side him, they both stopped dead in their tracks, dropping their packs in disbelief of what they saw in front of them.

Barely visible through it's hazy shroud, was a sight familiar to both of them. Draped in vines that attempted to swallow it, was a massive stone pyramid. The enormous structure looked identical to one Allison and Mya had climbed on a vacation in the Yucatan Peninsula. For some reason, Seth did not seem as surprised as the girls.

"It definitely does look like Mayan architecture, and just as deserted too." Noted Mya as they made their way toward the seemingly abandoned Temple.

As they neared the base, they were in awe from its size, it almost seemed larger than the ones they had seen in Southern Mexico. The corner stones had elaborate animal carvings engraved into them, which prompted Allison to say.

"You know what's really creepy? I haven't seen a single bug, snake, bird or any kind of animal since we got here. Did they all leave with the people that lived here? I guess a better question is why?"

Up to that point, there were no other visible structures, though some may have been covered with the choking vines that were everywhere. When they turned the corner of the pyramid, that all changed. Standing like permanent guards, were two rows of towering marble obelisks leading away from the steps of the pyramid. At least ten could be counted before they faded into the mist.

"Hey." Announced Allison. "I think I can put us on the map. The pyramid builders laid the foundations in a perfect north, south line, right? And being sun worshipers, it would make sense to orient the front of the pyramid due east. This looks like the front of it to me. Seth, which direction did we come from?"

Looking over his shoulder, he re-traced their trek in his mind, and pointed.

Referring back to the map, Allison drew a line with her finger from the original symbols.

"Obviously we don't know how far we have traveled, but based on the assumption that we now know which direction is east, and according to Seth's perfect memory, that should put us somewhere around here. We have been moving southeast from our starting point, which was Arizona, depending on how far we have come, that would very easily put us in Mexico. Or at least under Mexico."

"Which would explain the similar architecture here." Added Seth.

Mya and Allison were still amazed at the knowledge he had of their world, considering he had no contact with it up to this point.

Mya sketched a small pyramid on the map, south of the symbol that designated the FireStone mine, guessing the distance. There were some other markings close to the area, but had no way of knowing if it related to their current location.

"Well Allison, you suggested a hill to look from, I guess we had better start climbing." Remarked Mya.

"Me and my bright ideas." Allison mumbled as she raised her eyes towards the top of the stone staircase, there must have been hundreds of stairs. Mya grabbed her hand

and led her up the first few; Seth had taken the lead this time, anxious to get to the top. About half way up the side, Mya and Allison stopped to rest; their thighs were so tight, and burning from the climb, they had to take a break. Looking up the stairs, they could see Seth continuing on like a robot; the time alone gave them an opportunity to talk.

"Mya," Allison asked. "No one has really explained to me what is going on. What are we doing here? What are you doing?"

Mya sat silent for a moment, just staring off into the murky distance.

With a mild chuckle and a shake of her head, Mya answered.

"You know, I'm not really sure. This whole situation seems so surreal, yet, a part of me pulls at the very core of my soul with such confidence and power, that it feels like, well, maybe this is the piece of me I've been searching for."

Allison remained quiet, still confused, but as always, ready to support her best friend.

"I don't know how much Sinjin told you, but the reason he was looking for me, is because he is my grandfather, on my father's side. My father was charting these unusual sites when he died, and he wanted me to continue his work."

Allison had known Mya for many years, and although she had never admitted to her that not knowing her parents well, or their heritage bothered her, Allison could sense it. Maybe this was Mya's chance to answer the questions no one could help her with.

"How long are you going to do this? What about home?" Queried Allison.

"I want to finish my father's work to help Sinjin and the villagers, but I couldn't live there. As far as my job goes? I probably won't go back, I've earned all the money I need, plus it wouldn't be fair to the company. Being gone for so long, and then just showing up."

"What about you Allison? How are you doing with all of this?"

Smiling at her friend, and resting her cheek on her drawn up knees, she said.

"This is the best vacation I have ever taken with you. It's also the weirdest by far." Allison laughed.

"And, this is the first time we haven't been fighting over the guy!"

That got a giggle out of Mya.

"I can't believe you aren't interested in him Mya. He is so strong, and built. Have you seen those abs? Mmmm. You know I like my men tall too, he definitely has that going on. The long rock and roll hair might have to go though. His big perfect, white, smile, and those magnetic eyes that make you melt."

Mya laughed at her lusty infatuation.

"You sound like you're reading from a teen heart throb magazine."

"That teen magazine is quickly evolving into a 'dirty' magazine." Remarked Allison.

"When he touches me, even brushes against me, it's like an instant uncontrollable orgasm! Just like what people have told me about what you do to them. And that thing he did with me to give me energy? Woah! It wasn't just energy he gave me."

Allison found herself flush just reliving it in her mind.

"Seth was assigned to protect and teach me, it wouldn't be right to get involved that way. He is a hunk though, isn't he? Maybe we should catch up with him, let's go."

Chapter 23

The stairs seemed to go on forever, but finally they reached the summit. Instead of finding Seth waiting for them, he was kneeling inside the Temple doorway, immersed in prayer. The girls felt they should give him privacy, so they surveyed what they could from their perch.

As they walked all four sides of the top level, they strained to make out any distinct features through the mist, just shadows of the jungle that surrounded them. When they made their way back to the front, they sat on the edge and waited patiently for Seth. As they stared out into the hazy courtyard that led to the Temple, they tried to imagine what it must have been like to live here when it was occupied. How many people lived here? What caused them to leave? How did they build such a magnificent structure?

One thing that really puzzled them, was the material they used for the giant obelisks. It looked like polished black onyx, but where would they get such large amounts, and why not adorn the Temple with it as well? Did different people build different sections?

After what seemed to be an hour, Seth walked up behind the girls, he said nothing, but looked humble.

"Are you alright?" Asked Mya.

"I am fine." He responded.

"I have neglected my prayers."

Seth had been caught up in their adventures and was feeling guilty for not paying respect and giving thanks regularly.

"Did you see anything from up here Allison?" He asked.

"The only thing that I found, is that there is no breeze up here. Did you see if there was a way in? Maybe it's cooler inside?"

"Yes." Seth answered. "There is an entrance."

Getting up, Mya enthusiastically suggested they check it out.

There was no door at the entrance, just two pillars flanking a dark staircase; Mya suggested that Seth lead the way, since he had such good vision in the dark; she and Allison would follow behind, holding hands.

Allison's prediction, and hope was correct, the lava stone insulated the pyramid's interior from the hot sticky air that they had been trudging through. As they continued downward, the air become much cooler and more refreshing.

"Can you see anything Mya?" Whispered Allison.

"No." She replied.

The staircase was completely dark, but Mya knew from experience that Seth's vision in the dark was keen, and had the utmost confidence in him.

The passageway had several intersections, but Seth never hesitated trying to decide which one to take, it was if he knew where he was going, or someone was guiding him. Finally, after about the fifth intersection, Seth stopped and quietly announced that there was a light beginning to appear further down a narrow hallway.

"Is it another exit?" Asked Allison?

"I don't think so." Responded Seth. "I think there is a chamber ahead."

Creeping along the cold stone walls, like uninvited intruders, they slowly made their way to the illuminated chamber.

The room was not terribly bright, but still provided much more light than they had been used to in the passageways. Balanced atop several thin torches, were globes, glowing a pale white light. What they had expected to see, was possibly a burial chamber with mummies and trophies, but instead found the walls lined with thousands of books and paper scrolls, shelves lined with sculptures and artwork.

But as they quietly made their way into the room, another surprise waited for them.

"Do you hear that?" Whispered Seth, as he alerted the girls to a peculiar noise coming from the room. They nodded yes. Peering over a cluttered bookcase, they found a rather rotund man, splayed out on a chaise, snoring loudly, completely unaware of their presence.

"Should we wake him?" Whispered Allison.

But before anyone decided, the startled man jumped to his feet to see who had invaded his lair. His hearing was tremendously keen from living in isolation for years, their slightest whispers were like an alarm. Grabbing a long spear, and lunging forward, he shouted.

"Who goes there, and why?"

No one answered, so he bravely stepped forward and barked.

"I am Celton, now who are you?"

Mya sensed he was lying about his name, besides, what kind of name is 'Celton' anyway? Before she could answer, Seth stepped between them in a display of aggressive defense she had never witnessed.

"She is Mya, and she is a priestess and should be respected as such."

Allison looked at Mya and mouthed, "A priestess?"

Mya, just as surprised by Seth's announcement, shrugged her shoulders at her friend.

The once self-assured stranger, widened his eyes and glanced past the towering man that seemed to be guarding Mya.

"I know of a Mya, and she was the only one to have known how to find this place. How did you find your way in?" He asked.

Mya stepped around her protector.

"I have a key." She responded.

The man was much less defensive and said that only one person had such a key,

"Where did you get it from?" he skeptically asked.

"From my father, he left it for me."

Celton fell to his knees, partly in disbelief, but also from respect.

"It must be true then. I am a friend of your father's, I helped him seal the mine and keep intruders out until his return. Is he with you?"

"No," Mya added solemnly, "He passed on many years ago."

Celton's eyes looked at the ground in disbelief, he had waited for so long for his return.

Motioning him to his feet, Mya asked if they could all sit and talk. Allison grabbed her friend by the arm and whispered.

"Mya; a priestess ? What the hell was that all about?"

Mya just rolled her eyes and responded. "I'll explain it later."

Celton told how he had become friends with Mya's father while he was a prospector. When they had discovered the fire stone deposit, he agreed to keep it secret, and others away, until his return. Seth and Allison sat quietly as Celton described how much Mya's father talked of her. They also found out that his name was not Celton at all, but Michael. It was a last minute choice, it sounded more like a warrior's name than his own.

As it turns out, Michael was born in Ohio, but after a brief stint in college, and a failed marriage, he decided to roam the world in search of rare metals and stones. When he discovered this abandoned pyramid, he thought it would be a great place to stash his findings. He had collected everything from gold and silver, to rare crystals and of course, the FireStone.

"Want to see something really cool?" Michael offered.

"You obviously saw how this stone reacts to water, right? Now watch what it does with a magnet."

Michael pulled a small piece of FireStone from one pocket, and a flat magnetized, metal disc from the other. With some difficulty, he tied the two together, and with the expression of a magician, he took his hands away. Instead of dropping to the ground, the object just floated in front of them. Michael extended a finger, and gently nudged the hovering stone, causing it to effortlessly glide over to Mya.

"How does it work?" Asked Allison.

"Well, it basically allows the magnet to repel the earth's own magnetic radiation. No one has ever really explained it to me, but that's what I think."

Seth reached down, picked up a sizable rock, and

placed it on the flat disk; it held the weight, and gently carried it back over to Michael with the slightest push.

"Makes you wonder who else knew how to use it to move large objects."

"Or how many other things this FireStone can do." Allison replied.

"Michael, since you have been around here for awhile, and knew my father, do you think you can help us figure out where we are on this map?" Asked Mya, as she pulled it out and spread it on a table.

"Did you get this from your father?" He asked, as he traced a finger over different symbols and lines. Mya nodded yes, and then added.

"We don't have a legend that explains the symbols, do you know what they represent?" "Well, we are right here."

Pointing to a circle with two wavy lines inside it; the same area Allison had concluded.

"What does the symbol mean?" Repeated Mya.

"As you can see, there are only a few here on this map. Your father was searching for more of them, but I thought he was placing them on a different map, maybe he combined them. Anyway, these are gateways."

"Gateways?" Allison interrupted. "Gateways to where?

"To the other dimensions." Continued Michael.

"Parallel dimensions. It is believed that the builders and original occupants of this civilization moved there permanently."

Mya looked at Seth for any reaction; he didn't seem surprised, but offered no input.

A rather skeptical Allison asked.

"Have you ever traveled to one of these other dimensions Michael?"

"No, not yet." He replied, with a sly smile.

Allison pressed for more information.

"When you say other dimensions, do you mean spiritual, like when people die?"

"No. I'm talking about real, physical, places. Worlds that exist right here, in tandem with our own, we just can't see them." Michael tried to explain.

"Is that like the demonstration you gave me in the museum Seth?" Asked Mya.

"I believe it would be similar, as far as understanding how it would exist, but when we shifted to another plane, we were in our own dimension, not another world. I think you would have to use a gateway for that." Speculated Seth.

"So why haven't you gone through a gateway yet Michael?" Mya asked.

"Because I don't know how. I think your father knew, but he did not tell me."

"If you have never gone through one, then what makes you so sure there are other dimensions?" Asked Allison.

"There are thousands of references and suggestions throughout history, and things I have seen. I have also read a great deal, as you can see." As Michael pointed to the thousands of books and manuscripts on the shelves and tables.

"What have you seen that makes you believe that it's possible to travel to these other dimensions?" Asked Seth.

Michael thought for a moment, unsure of whether he should reveal a secret to them. Then the sly smile returned as he said.

"Follow me."

Leading them through a narrow passageway away from his library, the chubby little recluse explained that what he was about to show them, was here when he discovered this place.

The humidity and temperature was rising rapidly, obviously they were headed outside again.

"There it is; I call her Mable. Once I figure out how, I'm going to take her for a spin through a gateway." Announced Michael, as they emerged into an outdoor courtyard. In front of them, rested a large, circular craft.

"A flying saucer?" Shouted Allison.

"Well, a saucer I guess, I've never seen it fly." Laughed Michael. "I think it must have broken down, which is why it was left behind."

"Okay, so you think these gateways are used by aliens for interplanetary travel? Like the worm hole theories?" Quipped Allison.

"Nah." Replied Michael. "You want to know my theory? I don't think interplanetary travel is realistic. It doesn't make sense, you couldn't go fast enough to get anywhere, plus I don't think anyone could survive the radiation belts. I think that these craft are from right here on Earth. Just being built by people in other dimensions. They come through the gateways to visit, or study our civilizations, and then go back. Maybe they are inter-dimensional tourists."

"Well, it certainly seems possible." Mya added.

"Can we go inside?" Asked an excited Seth.

"Sure." Michael said, motioning them to follow him.

A sliding hatch appeared to be the only way in, Michael had placed a stone block below it to serve as a step. Mya touched the craft's side as she prepared to step onto the block. It was not made of metal, but felt more like a plastic. It was a pale gray color, until her hand touched it, then it began changing to the color of her skin. She could also feel a very faint vibration that slightly tickled the palm of her hand. When she removed her hand, it changed back to it's original gray color.

"Weird, huh." Said Michael. "It somehow changes color to match whatever it comes in contact with. Here watch."

Michael grabbed a large leaf from a nearby plant, and held it to the craft's hull. Once again, the gray faded into a rich green, blending perfectly with the leaf.

"It's some kind of organic camouflage." Said Allison.

Stepping inside, Seth was surprised at how much room there was inside, his tall frame could actually stand up straight. There were a few seats around, and large windows all around the walls, and even below their feet, like a glass bottom boat. What was odd, was there were no signs of windows from the outside. In the center of the craft, was a seat and desk. Near the edge of the desk, were two pads, spaced about two feet apart.

Seth could not resist the temptation of sitting at the desk. Setting his pack on the floor, he slid into the seat, which was designed for someone a bit smaller than he, but that didn't bother him, and placed both of his hands on the pads. To everyone's surprise, except Michael, the desktop lit up. There was a myriad of illuminated signs, lines and symbols that made no sense.

"This is where I run into problems." Explained Michael. "I can't decipher the language, I have a few books written in the same words, but don't have anyway to translate them."

Seth's eyes glanced up at Mya to see her reaction. As she looked closer, she whispered in Seth's ear.

"This is the same language inscribed on the gold walls we found in your Temple's secret chamber. Remember? Can you read it?"

"No, I can't read it. It is a very ancient and sacred language." He whispered back.

The brightly colored desktop faded to black about thirty seconds after Seth removed his hands from the pads.

The once skeptical Allison, was quickly becoming convinced that Michael's theory may be right.

"This wouldn't have been used for long journeys." She concluded. "Look, there are no places to sleep. If they were traveling a great distance, they would have to have beds. Right?"

It made sense to everyone else.

"When you learn how to operate this vehicle, I would gladly accompany you on your journey to another dimension, if you would like a companion."

Seth offered. His desire for adventure had not diminished.

"Thank you Seth, I would welcome the company."

As they were leaving the craft, Mya turned to Michael.

"I almost forgot, my father had a stone key, that was believed to have been hidden in the mine. It is the only key known to be able to de-activate all of the portals at once. Do you have any idea what it looks like, or where it may be hidden?"

Michael thought for a moment, and then said.

"I don't know of a hidden key, but you father did give me a carved stone, that must have had some amount of importance, he asked me to keep an eye on it for him until his return. It's in my library."

Allison was happy to be back in the coolness of the library, the humidity seemed to sap her strength very quickly. She and Seth were studying all of the book titles while Michael searched for the stone he had been entrusted with.

Seth dreamed of having his own library someday; it must be wonderful to have so many books at your disposal.

There were books in all types of languages, and on all subjects. Great literary classics, and obscure textbooks from libraries and universities around the world.

"How did you get these books?" Allison asked.

"Oh, I've borrowed them from various places."

Answered Michael, as he rummaged through drawers and crates, searching for the stone.

"But they come from every corner of the earth. How did you travel so much?"

"I used the portals to take me where I wanted to go, picked out what I wanted, and made my way back here. There might be a few that are overdue though." Michael chuckled.

"I found it!" Exclaimed Michael. "I was beginning to get worried, but here it is. I guess you can have it, since your father isn't coming back. I don't know if it is what you are looking for, but here, it's yours now."

Mya took the stone from his hand, it did not look like a traditional key, but more like the one she had been using to activate the sleds. The major difference, was that it was hewn from brown marble, polished, and had an emerald scarab inset in the middle of the eight sided stone.

All four of them huddled around the map, in search of a symbol with a scarab, but none could be found.

The Temple of The Ancients would be the only location that would have that specific symbol, and in order to de-activate all of the portals at once, they had to find it.

Mya pulled out all of the maps and journals from her pack, and spread them out.

"Look at all of the maps, maybe he had a separate one, as Michael was saying, that he marked with a scarab."

Mya knew that the scarab beetle was used as an ancient Egyptian talisman, and finally decided to look for an area on the map that might correlate to Egypt. Nothing seemed to point to Egypt, and there were no signs of a scarab anywhere on any of the maps. Maybe the stone had nothing to do with the key they had been searching for. Everyone had lain down to take a break, and clear their minds, except Seth. He was determined to solve the puzzle.

Although there were no geographic boundaries drawn on the maps, everyone had agreed they knew where Egypt was.

Seth began looking at the various symbols and the pattern they created in that area. He started thinking about the constellations, and how the Greeks had drawn images in the sky, by connecting the stars together. What if he connected the symbols together? Would they point him in the right direction? After several different combinations, one seemed to stick out. He traced it over and over again in his mind and then asked everyone.

"How many legs would a scarab have?"

"Beetles are insects, so it would have six legs. Why?" Responded Allison.

"I think I may have found it."

The others got to their feet to see what Seth had come up with.

He continued, drawing imaginary lines, connecting symbols in the area.

"Just like a constellation, if you make a line here, and here, then connect these, it looks like a scarab with six legs. In the center of the body is a symbol of a gateway and a portal. I think this is it." Declared Seth.

"It's the only clue we have. I think we should try." Added Mya.

"Michael, where is the portal that you use, could you take us there?"

"Certainly Mya." He responded. "It is actually in the chamber above us."

"Well, let's gather the maps up, and get going." She said. Mya was never one to procrastinate. 'Do it now, or don't complain when you don't have time later.' was one of her mottoes. Allison was tired of all of the walking and all of the stairs, but she knew better than to complain, besides, her competitive nature would never allow her to show Mya any weakness. Fortunately, the trip was indeed short. The portal chamber was exactly the same as the others they had been to, but now, they knew how to control their destination. This was Allison's first trip through a portal, and was a bit nervous, so she stuck pretty close to Seth. Michael helped them lower the crystal capped poles into place, leaving one up.

"I'll lower the last one when you are all on the pedestal." Offered Michael.

Seth and Allison climbed onto the pedestal, Mya walked over to Michael.

"Michael, thank you for your loyalty to my father, and guarding this place for so long. Now that you know I have the key, do you plan on staying here, or move on?"

"I have been here a long time, I think I will continue trying to get Mable flying. I'll probably do a bit more prospecting; I miss that. I do hope to see you again somewhere."

With a strong hug, she wished him safety and prosperity and joined the others on the pedestal, and set the stone key in it's place.

"Thank you so much for your help Michael." Yelled Mya; then waved goodbye. Seth, Mya and Allison began focusing and concentrating on the symbol of the location they wanted, and Mya turned the key.

Michael lowered the last pole, which caused all of them to light up. As the rays of light focused on the trio, Michael waved and said,.

"God's speed; be safe."

They were gone before the last word fell from his lips.

Chapter 24

Allison wasn't sure what had happened, there was a bright flash of light, then, the room went back to normal. The only thing different, was that Michael was no longer there. Seth, however, pointed to the symbol in front of them; it was now the one they had wanted. The portal worked properly. He quickly hopped down and raised one of the poles to prevent it from starting the process over again. There was only one exit from the room they were in, so they made their way through it until they reached a room that connected to several tunnels. Seth and Mya had faced the same situation before, however this time there were no markings above any of the tunnels, they had no idea which one to take.

"If we are indeed in the Temple of The Ancients, I think we should look for a ceremonial chamber. Controlling all of the portals would have been done from a special location, not in public view." Suggested Seth.

"But how do we know which tunnel would take us there? We could be lost forever if it's a labyrinth." Noted Allison.

"The Elders and the Ancients will guide us, just as Kira said they would. We must meditate and ask for their assistance, they know the way." Said Seth, as he sat on the ground in preparation. Allison was not convinced, but she was in no position to argue with them, so she sat down next to them.

"Mya," Seth instructed, "you must practice and learn to talk with the Ancients also, you are their descendant, a direct link to this physical world, their future, our future. They welcome you."

Mya was eager to learn how to tap into this infinite fountain of knowledge and experience she had been told about. Part of her was skeptical, but she also believed that if she had any doubts, she would never be able to focus enough to be successful. Sitting a few feet away from Allison and Seth, Mya leaned against a wall, taking the load of her pack off of her back, and closed her eyes. She really didn't know what to do or think of, she began thinking in terms of prayer, but feelings of guilt and thoughts of blasphemy clouded her concentration. Would God think she was praying to her ancestors for guidance rather than Him? That was not her intent, and made a short prayer to appease her conscience, then cleared her mind and tried to focus on the goal, rather than the process. Soon, her mind was wandering to all kinds of subjects and memories, which she deliberately tried to suppress, but with little success. Though she felt undisciplined enough to keep a clear mind, she was feeling more relaxed, and finally succumbed to her random thoughts; surely Seth would be more successful. Mya tried visualizing herself standing in front of a room full of wise men and women, like a Roman Senate floor or something, asking for direction, but eventually her thoughts turned to her childhood, people she missed, mostly her mother.

She remembered sentimental moments, baking breads at Christmas time, helping in the garden, asking advice on boys. Her mother always made her make her own decisions, giving her the confidence to stand on her own, and either bear the burden of a hasty choice, or reap the rewards of a good decision.

"Follow your gut, it understands more than your head." She used to tell her, and, "You will never regret having worked hard for something, anyone can take the easy road." Words that Mya used to roll her eyes at as a child, but also words that built a work ethic envied by her professional peers. Her gut instinct had served her well in business, in fact it was extremely rare when she was wrong, maybe someone had been guiding her all along.

Mya opened her eyes and looked at all of her choices, stood up and then slowly walked by the entrance to each tunnel, finally stopping at the mouth of the one that was closest to the one they had recently emerged from. She did not say anything, just stood in there silently, staring into the blackness. Seth finally opened his eyes to see Mya standing in front of the tunnel he was about to suggest.

Walking up behind her, he asked.

"Did the Ancients tell you this was the one? This is the one I was told."

"No." Mya explained. "I wasn't able to reach them, I just remembered my mother telling me to rely on my instincts, which led me here."

"But Mya, they reached you. Your mother helped you, she is one your ancestors, and she knew how to help you."

If Mya had realized her mother was speaking to her, she would have tried to respond to her; she hoped she would have another chance.

"Well, if you both agree, lets get this over with and find what we are looking for." Interrupted Allison.

The tunnel they had chosen, was narrow, dark and steep. After a few minutes of ascending, they reached a dead end, Mya couldn't believe that they had both chosen the wrong tunnel, but sure enough, a solid wall stood in their path. Mya stepped back and searched the walls with the beam of her flashlight, which was slowly getting dimmer, in hopes of any clues.

Allison had been pushing on the stone that blocked their passage, hoping that a burst of Herculean strength would move it; it never budged. In frustration, Allison kicked dirt against it, like the manager of a baseball team towards an unsympathetic umpire. The dust created a cloud that they all choked on, until Seth pointed out that some of the dust did not curl back towards them, but was escaping upwards. Mya shone the light toward the sloping ceiling, indeed there was an opening. Everyone had been so convinced it was a dead end, nobody looked up. The opening was about eight feet from the ground, so Seth acted as a platform to push the girls up first, they would help him up last. Mya was first, once there she confirmed that it was another path, or a continuation of the same one.

"It's like a vertical switchback, to throw people off, come on up." She said. Allison made it up easily, then Seth jumped up and grabbed the upper ledge, wedging his long legs against the walls while the girls grabbed whatever they could of him to hoist him up. They were all hoping the corridor would lead them straight to the chamber, but were disappointed again when they ran into another wall, this time, however, they quickly looked for a hidden passage. The ceiling did not reveal any openings as before, so they scoured the walls and even backtracked a little looking for clues.

Seth's attention soon turned to the floor, perhaps there was a trap door that they had walked across and not realized it. He found no trap door, but did notice something unusual along one section of the floor where the wall met it, and called the girls over to get their opinion. What he had discovered, was lines of dirt that had accumulated over time, from something being moved across the floor. By following the faint scars, they could tell where the door was, or at least should be. Mya's flashlight was becoming so dim, it was difficult to see any details at all. Running their hands along the walls, everyone looked for a button, hinges, a handle or some clue. Finally Allison found a seam in the wall that ran from floor to ceiling, and ran her finger along it to make it more visible. Mya and Seth came over to inspect it, it was obviously a door, but how did it open? After much discussion and frustration, Seth noticed a rope tucked along the floor's edge on the opposite wall, he called the girls over to help him pull. Allison positioned herself closest to the wall, placed her foot against it and pulled with all her might. Mya was behind her, and Seth tugging on the end. The rope seemed to be attached to a weighted pulley system that pulled the door open. As the door began to slide open, a warm light began to filter in behind them.

Once the opening was wide enough to pass through they stopped pulling, only to realize that the door began to close immediately, somehow they would need to find a way to prop it open. The three of them continued pulling until Seth was inside the doorway, where he found a post to lash the rope to, preventing the door from closing.

Exhausted from pulling, the girls joined Seth in the doorway, where he basked in the glow emanating from the sacred chamber they had been searching for. Slowly, and cautiously, they walked into a room that was intricately decorated with gold and silver walls and ceilings, inlaid with delicate patterns of lapis lazuli and opal. In the center was an elaborate altar carved of polished marble and two symbols engraved into it's top. In front of the altar, set into the wall, was a large piece of glass, resembling a leaded glass window, the light that filled the room was coming from it. The glass was etched with an assortment of lines and symbols that were all to familiar with them, Mya's father's map matched it.

There was another smaller chamber off to the right, it was a portal, like all the others. Eventually Mya made it to the altar to see if she could figure out what they needed to do in order to close the portals. The symbol on the right was the common marking for the portals, and to the left, was the symbol for the gateways. Between them was a depression for the stone key Michael had given her, and the same slot that holds the brass template used at the Fire-Stone deposit, apparently you needed both of them to make it work. Seth suggested they might be able to still use the portal, since they had a key, to get back home after they used the master key to close the rest. Allison thought it was a good idea to figure out which symbol on the map would get them home, before they got carried away; so they unfolded the map once again to locate their destination. There was a portal near Mt. Ranier, in Washington, that should be close enough; of course there was the one in the Temple at Seth's village, but bringing Allison there would be forbidden. They would take a plane to Redding and then drive to Mt. Shasta.

Seth and Allison stood by the entrance of the portal, while Mya set the template and then the key in place. The key was pointing towards the portal symbol, and was just getting ready to turn it to the neutral position, when a loud, unfamiliar voice shouted 'No!'

A startled Mya turned around to see a Traveler, walking through the door they had propped open.

"You were not supposed to find that, give it to me." He demanded, as he pointed to the metal plate.

"He must have been the one that ransacked your apartment." Yelled Allison. "That is what he was looking for."

Mya's eyes glanced at Seth, and he moved his eyes over to the glass wall. She took his clue, and turned the key all the way to the left so it was pointing at the gateway symbol. Suddenly, the scarab lit up, and the glass wall turned into a brilliant green.

The Traveler was surprised and turned to look at it. Seth took a fast run at him and hit him like a well trained linebacker, knocking him into the gateway. Mya and Allison were shocked by his aggressiveness, but thankful.

The Traveler disappeared into the gateway, and Seth fell to the ground.

"Quick, turn the key to shut off the gateway." He yelled, getting to his feet. Mya turned the stone key back to the center position, causing the glass wall to return to it's normal state.

"Let's get to the portal before he finds his way back."" Said Mya as she pulled the key and template out.

"I sure hope this works." Remarked Allison.

"We know where we want to go…now everyone focus."

Allowing themselves about fifteen seconds to concentrate on their objective, Mya turned the key, the familiar blue light surrounded them, and they were at their destination. When the light faded, the ring of staffs that pointed at the platform, automatically retreated into their place in the walls, indicating that it was locked after their use. They had done it; no one could use it without a key. A bit out of breath, and with their hearts pounding from excitement, they started up the corridor that would lead them to the surface. Allison seemed more concerned than the others, about being followed again by the Traveler, she was more than ready for her 'normal' life.

Chapter 25

The air became more damp and sweeter smelling, indicating they were near the surface. Mya was the first to emerge from the camouflaged tunnel entrance, only to begin chuckling.

"Wouldn't you figure? My first time visiting Washington, and it's raining!"

Allison didn't care, at least they were above ground, and they were somewhere recognizable, Seth was thrilled with the constant drops hitting his face, rain was still a novelty to him. The trek down the mountain was cold and wet, but everyone was so glad to breathe the fresh air, they didn't seem to mind. When they finally made it to a road, they stuck their thumbs out in hopes for catching a ride into town. Car after car passed them by. Mya felt like cursing the unconcerned motorists as they sped past them, but knew that she had passed many hitch hikers herself out of fear of the worst. Eventually, a large, covered stake bed truck pulled to the side of the road; Mya stepped up to the cab to be greeted by an older man in coveralls.

"You look mighty soaked ma'am." He said.

"The name's Bart, and I'm headed to the market in Seattle, where are you going?"

"That would be perfect." Mya responded.

"You'll all have to ride in the back, it may not be warm, but it's drier and faster than walking. Sorry, but I just don't let hitch hikers up front." He added.

"I understand, we appreciate the help." Said Mya, as she waived her partners on. The soggy trio climbed into the bed amongst some boxes of vegetables, and tried to relax on the ride into town. They must have all dozed off, because the next thing they knew, Bart was telling them to get out, they were at the market place. In appreciation, they helped him unload the boxes and crates onto a cart, and then made their way into the market.

"Do we have any cash left?" Asked Allison. " I am really hungry, and this fish looks great."

"Yeah." Mya said. "Let's eat."

After walking through all of the flower stands and bakeries, they settled on a little restaurant that didn't seem to care if the patrons were in wet clothes.

Seth loved all of the activity going on around him, the smells of the salt air, the fresh pastries and breads. All three of them enjoyed a steaming bowl of clam chowder that warmed them up nicely. Mya and Seth each ordered grilled salmon, while Allison requested a large lobster. Seth had never seen one before, and wasn't too keen on it when it came to the table. He said it looked like a giant bug.

It was obvious that Mya had assumed a leadership role within the trio, one that she had not wanted, but fit naturally.

"We need to get back to Shasta; to show our find to Kira, and so Allison can get her car and her life back. Let's get a plane flight out of here tomorrow."

Seth was noticeably nervous as they entered the airport terminal, so many people scurrying about. He stood by the large glass windows, and watched the large metallic birds scream skyward, while Mya purchased the tickets. It was an early flight, so there was no problem getting seats for all three. Seth had to hunch over to walk down the aisle. Pointing him to a window seat, Allison followed in behind him to sit in the next seat.

"Here, let me put this on you," She said, as she leaned over to fasten his seatbelt. Allison lingered awhile, as she the goosebumps grew on her arm, she still had a crush on him. Mya sat in the same row, but across the aisle.

"How we doing over there?" She asked. Seth looked back with a very nervous, but large grin. Allison held his hand for comfort.

As the jet raced down the runway, Seth couldn't take his eyes away from the window, they were moving so fast it worried him. Then, the nose pointed upward and they were airborne. Allison thought her hand would be crushed, as Seth tightened his grip while witnessing the ground falling away.

Once they had reached altitude, Seth proudly commented.

"We are flying with the clouds."

"They look very different from above, don't they?"

Mya asked, as she strained to look out a window. The flight was fairly uneventful, until they began their descent, where the plane had to fly through a storm. Just as he had begun to feel comfortable with flight, Seth felt uneasy, as the picturesque view faded to the milky soup of a storm cloud. The plane began to tip and bounce as the turbulence increased. Allison noticed the queasy look on his face and quickly grabbed an air sickness bag. The thought of him hurling all over the place nearly made her gag as well. Allison was quite the veteran when it came to air travel, and had mastered the motion sickness problems Seth was encountering, but we he could control it no more, he had to use the bag. All of her experience could not help her stop the contagious feeling that was now making her grab for a bag.

The plane touched down smoothly in Redding and taxied over to it's gate, all the while Allison was trying to pretend that she hadn't just filled the paper bag. Seth asked. "What should I do with this?"

Holding his bag up. Allison started dry heaving uncontrollably again.

Though empathetic for them, Mya couldn't help but chuckle, they both looked so miserable.

Chapter 26

The drive was relaxing for all of them, Seth was especially glad to be back on solid ground, Allison was sound asleep in the back seat. The scenery was becoming more familiar and comforting to Seth, more tall trees and brisker air. The majestic snow capped mountain that sat over his village, stood out like a towering sanctuary, it's no wonder his ancestors selected it for their colony.

Pulling off of the freeway, My announced that they were back in the town Mt. Shasta.

"Wake up sleepy head, let's get something to eat before going to Sinjin's."

The menu at the small diner did little to entice Allison; her stomach was still on the plane. Mya and Seth, however, had no trouble devouring a greasy cheeseburger with a thick slice of onion, and a pile of fries. Seth had learned to love the food he had never seen before; he would miss it.

The long winding drive out to Sinjin's cabin was the perfect opportunity for Mya to explain to Allison, as much of the priestess thing as she understood. She also explained that Allison would have to go home, not continue with them to the village. As much as Mya had thought she wanted to, Allison was ready to get back to a normal life.

"Don't worry, I'm not staying there either. Once we have done what Kira asked, I'll be calling and telling you that I'm headed home."

The rest of the drive was quiet, Allison was worried about not having her friend around, and Mya was wondering if she would be able to have her old life back. She didn't want to be a priestess, she had wrestled with odd things all her life, she didn't need that burden too. Seth had grown fond of Allison, and had a bit of a crush on her as well, but he knew that a relationship could not work.

The small cabin finally came into view, Allison's car still parked on the side where she had left it.

"I don't think I'll come in," Allison stated. "I'll say my good-bye's here." Remembering the last time she was in the cabin.

Hugs, tears, and promises of future reunions, ended as Mya's closest and dearest friend drove away.

Shastina did not greet them at the porch as she did last time. Instead, they knocked on the door several times. After a few moments of waiting, the door creaked open and Shastina motioned them in, she looked unusually tired.

Following her into Sinjin's study, they quickly realized why. The once strong, and confident man, was lying on his bed, pale and weak. Shastina had not slept since he became ill.

"What is wrong Sinjin?" Mya asked as she knelt by his side. Reaching his wrinkled hand out to comfort her, he replied.

"I am old, this body of mine is preparing to give out."

"He has had a fever as well, I think that has weakened him more than his age." Shastina added.

In an effort to cheer him up, Mya explained,

"We found the FireStone deposit that my father discovered. We are taking it to Kira."

Sinjin's eyes did light up at the news.

"I need to go back to my village, I will journey with you."

"But you are too weak to travel." Seth was concerned for the venerable old man.

"Our ancestors and our Creator will give me the strength I need."

"I think seeing his people will do him wonders," Shastina whispered. "Their healers can do more for him than I can."

"Well, let's get a good nights rest and head out tomorrow morning."

That evening, Mya joined Seth in his rituals and prayers, something he had never included her in before. He felt that she needed to learn.

At bed time, Seth and Mya knelt on either side of Sinjin's bed, reaching across her grandfathers body, clasped hands with Seth. Together, they began to concentrate and focus as much energy as they could, in hopes that they could transfer some of theirs into Sinjin. Mya soon was aware that she could feel her grandfather's life force, which had a tempo much like her own. She concentrated on matching that frequency, and soon, Seth had picked up on it as well. Instantly she could feel wave after wave of intense energy flowing back and forth between the three of them. The drain on her was taking its toll and she let go of Set's hands, the exchange had been broken.

"I need a break." She confessed.

"I think he will be better by morning, let's go to sleep

now." Seth concluded.

Sinjin was up before anyone else, preparing a small pack of his own. He definitely looked as though he felt better.

"Let us go now," Sinjin ordered as they finished their breakfast. Seth quickly picked up the Elder's pack.

"I will carry this for you." He would have disgraced himself to let someone of his position carry their own pack, plus he was honored to do so.

Mya felt sad for Shastina, she would not make the trip, she was to stay behind and take care of Rolex.

"Please take good care of Sinjin, I hope to see him again soon."

The loneliness in her eyes was already showing. Mya assured her that she would.

Blazing the trail like an adventurer a third of his age, Sinjin looked strong again. The thought of seeing his people, old friends and the fact his granddaughter was traveling with him, invigorated him.

As a child, Mya had often dreamed about spending time with the man she had never met, but even her dreams would have never taken her down this path. Seth had wanted to talk with Sinjin about his adventures and journeys, the stories every child in the village told, but respectfully, walked behind the two as they got to know each other.

The pace began to slow as they neared the secret entrance, Sinjin was weakening, soon he was stopping more often.

"We must get him to the healers soon, if I have to carry him on my back, I will." Seth exclaimed. The old man refused the piggy back ride, but was able to gather enough strength to continue after a brief rest.

Chapter 27

The valley below was a welcome site for all of them, but particularly Sinjin, not only was he weakening, but it had been many years since his return. He steadied himself with his walking stick, as they navigated the narrow path down to the small meadow. The soft ground was much kinder on his aching feet than the rocky path had been. They made their way back to the Temple of Elders and settled onto one of the benches.

"I will got to the neighboring village and tell them of your arrival, and bring the healers back with me."

Seth turned to head out of the Temple, when he noticed Mya's expression change to concern. She nervously looked around them, when Seth asked her what was wrong.

"Burnt molasses." She tensely answered.

Seth wasn't quite sure what she meant, until he saw something that stopped him in his tracks. Standing in the doorway, blocking his exit, was a Traveler. Seth was startled, but did not move, he did not want the Traveler to think he was afraid, and he also wanted to protect Sinjin and Mya. Mya stood up and slowly walked to Seth's side in a show of solidarity and courage.

"What is it that you want here?" Sinjin bellowed from his seated position."

Mya wasn't certain how the Traveler would respond, as its face was smooth and without a mouth.

"I mean you no disrespect, and am hear to clear up a matter that has gotten out of control."

The words were very clear, but seemed to come from its chest, rather than where its mouth should be.

"I have something that belongs to you." Another Traveler appeared from outside the temple door, and handed the other one a wooden box. The Traveler stepped toward them, and set the box at their feet. Cautiously, Seth bent down and lifted the lid.

"The Knowledge Crystal!" Seth exclaimed.

It was not nearly as large as Mya had anticipated. Along side it were all of the missing maps. Sinjin stood and came forward. "Why did you steal it from us?"

"We did not steal it, it was taken by one of your own people, to bargain with."

Seth was stunned, as was Sinjin. Why would anyone from the village take it from their own people?

"I am returning it in good faith."

"And what of the Elders that you took?" Mya added.

"They were taken until we found out who from your village had taken our FireStone, we only have one. Your Elders will be returned immediately."

Still confused as to who would do it, but why? Everyone wondered, what were they bargaining for?

"One of your people knew that we had a FireStone, and assumed we knew where it could be mined. In exchange for that information, he tried to offer us your maps and Knowledge Crystal. When he realized we did not know where the mine was, he stole the stone. We have it back now, and we have the person that took it." Announced the Traveler.

"Where is this traitor that has caused so much fear and pain?" Mya said angrily.

"He awaits you in the courtyard." Responded the Traveler, as he stepped aside the doorway.

Mya stopped at the top of the Temple stairs with Seth and Sinjin close behind. In front of them was a young man, kneeling, with his forehead touching the ground.

"Lemule?" Seth said.

A soft, humble voice responded.

"It is I. I cannot look upon you, I have disgraced you all."

Taking a few steps down the stairs, a disbelieving Seth scoured.

"You are the one who betrayed us? Why would you do such a thing?"

Lemule finally looked up at his childhood friend.

"Because of you." He admitted.

"Me? How is it you have done something so foul, and yet blame me for you actions?"

Mya had never seen Seth so angry to raise his voice.

"You had all of the glory; I should have been chosen for the journey. If I had delivered the whereabouts of the FireStone mine, the Elders would have favored me for a change. I did not believe them when they told me they did not know, so I took the items and told everyone that the Traveler's had stolen them."

It was hard for Seth to hear of Lemule's jealousy of him. He thought of him as a friend, not a competitor.

"So when the Traveler came up from the lake, he was looking for you, and when you disappeared in the portal, you were running away." Mya accused.

"It is true." He said as he lowered his head in shame.

Mya turned to the Traveler.

"We owe you our deepest apologies, and our appreciation for setting this matter straight."

Sinjin was proud as he listened to his granddaughter acting as an official village leader.

"Lemule, you shall answer to the Council tomorrow." Sinjin ordered.

"I will go and release your Elders now." Said the Traveler as he walked away with the other one.

"And I shall go to the other village and bring Kira and the others back." Volunteered Seth. As the two Travelers walked across the courtyard, Mya got another whiff of the very distinct odor that was always present around them.

She remembered how they tried to prevent her from finding the mine and the scarab stone. Something inside of her did not trust their 'gesture of good faith'. She knew there was something else to their story, but decided to hold off on any accusations.

The village was quite a different scene now, with all of the residents back. Mya was seated next to Kira, as Sinjin took his place of honor with the other Elders of the Council, Seth remained outside, since he was not one of the Elders, and did not hold any high positions. Instead, he stayed in the courtyard and kept the children spellbound with tales of their travels. The young ones would tell his stories over and over again, exaggerating a little more each time, placing him in legendary status.

Lemule was brought in to answer to the Elders, standing silently as the charges of betrayal were levied against him, he hung his head in shame. After admitting to what he had done, Kira stood and announced his punishment.

"Lemule, because you have endangered so many here, falsely accused another people of your wrong doings, it saddens me to have you banished from our community, but you have left us know choice. Our neighboring villages will be told of your punishment, it will be their decision if they let you stay with them. I wish you good health, and understanding Lemule."

When Kira sat down, Lemule slowly turned, accepting his punishment, and walked out. Mya felt sorry for him, yet understood the need for the banishment.

As he left the courtyard heading for the edge of the village, he heard that laughter of children, they were all gathered around Seth, lauding him like a hero. It felt like salt in his wounds, he still wanted to be in Seth's place. Seth never saw his old friend leaving.

Although the day started out on a somber note, the afternoon was filled with celebration. Lots of dancing and music along with a large feast. Mya was treated as royalty by all, and was told many times that she had a place of prestige here in the village. Mya was torn for a direction, she had longed for a family, a history and a purpose, and here it was for her. However, she missed her life on the surface. While many here enjoyed condemning the ways of the 'moderns', she could not turn her back on her friends, like Allison, or cars and fancy restaurants, she liked being able to watch a movie or go to the theater. Mya understood that she did not live in a perfect world, but she now had some tools to make better sense of it.

"I have been so honored and fortunate to have met you all, I have learned so much. I know I have much more to learn, but I don't think I will stay." Announced Mya.

Sinjin and Kira were disappointed, but expected the decision.

"I would, however, like to continue my father's work,

and returning on occasion to share my findings with you."

"Your father would be as proud of your choice as I am." Sinjin answered.

Seth had been standing nearby, and was hoping she would stay. Sinjin turned to him and said.

"Seth, I will need a replacement for myself soon, if you continue the Higher Studies, I want it to be you."

Seth was humbled, and very excited by the offer. This was a huge announcement and honor. His short, but exciting time on the surface had only increased his taste for adventure.

"I will study ever so hard. Thank you." Replied Seth.

"Mya, I know you are anxious to get home, so I will have Seth accompany you to my cabin tomorrow. I will be staying a while longer. I will miss you."

Mya could not keep the tears in, and quickly gave her recently found grandfather a tight hug.

The goodbye at Sinjin's cabin was very difficult, Mya knew there was a good chance she would never see Seth again.

"If you come back and see me, I promise to buy you an ice cream cone." She said in a joking bribe.

"I have a present for you, hold out your hand. You said you have a szja?" Asked Mya.

"At my home in the village, yes."

"Then please put this in it."

Seth was surprised and pleased to see Mya's little photograph that had been in her szja.

"Thank you Mya, I will cherish it."

Mya didn't even try to hold back the tears as Shastina drove her back to the little town with such a big secret.

It had been two months since Mya had left her people. She quit her job, she had made enough money from her last deal to last a very long time, and was preparing to embark on her new life journey, finding the places her father was looking for.

Sitting in her living room, studying a book on mystical symbols, her phone rang. A familiar voice on the other end simply said, "Everyone needs a travel companion." and then hung up. The click of the receiver was quickly followed by a knock on the door.

Peering out the peephole, she saw no one, assuming it was a delivery, she opened the door to see, sitting patiently on the doormat; Rolex, Sinjin's dog.